*For Hannah Raines and Shyla Martin, my college friends who took an "epic" roadtrip with me. Though we haven't seen each other in years, you and those memories made, stick with me forever!*

With summer sun, a girls' trip, and enough romance to leave a smile on your face, *Destination: Romance* is the perfect vacation. And you don't even have to pack for the trip!

— HEATHER GREER, TWO-TIME SELAH AWARD FINALIST

A chance encounter on a road trip kicks off the perfect summer read. Destination: Romance combines flirty fun with deeper spiritual themes to create a compelling and satisfying book you won't want to put down.

— ELIZABETH MADDREY, USA TODAY BESTSELLING AUTHOR OF THE BILLIONAIRE'S NANNY

Roadtrip Romance • Book One

# AMY R. ANGUISH

# 1

F ive to one, their team, Camden Malone readied to serve. He reared back, aimed … but his eyes strayed toward a brunette just entering the pool area.

*Wham!*

"Watch out!"

Too late.

The ball careened out of the pool and smacked the very source of his distraction in the side of the head. A small *oof* escaped the perfectly shaped lips as the impact rocked her whole body. Her flipflop clad foot slipped on the edge of the pool, and what had been totally embarrassing turned catastrophic. One of those moments where time slowed to make each instant feel eternal.

He dove two seconds too late. Her body smacked the water and sank. Pushing himself beneath the surface, Camden fumbled to grasp her as she fought against him, walloping his cheek and elbowing him in the ribs. He finally got a solid enough grip to stand and lift both their heads into the blessed oxygen.

"Let go of me!" She coughed and wiggled.

"I was just trying to help." He shifted his hands as she continued squirming so much, he was afraid he might drop her.

"I wasn't drowning. I just lost my balance because some goon in the pool hit me with his ball." She brushed several waterlogged strands of brown curls out of her hazel eyes and blinked at him. "You." Her short legs kicked harder.

"I'm sorry. I wasn't aiming at you." He wasn't ready to relinquish her from his arms.

"Well, you need to work on your aim." She pushed against his chest, her hands unintentionally sending pleasure through his skin.

"You caught a feisty one there, Cam!" His cousin Ryan guffawed from the other side of the pool. "She might be *too* much fish. Throw her back."

"Can you stop wiggling for a minute so I can make sure you're okay?"

"Why? Are you a doctor or something?" She caught him with her elbow.

"I have a degree in physical therapy and am a trained life-guard, actually."

She stilled. "Oh."

"Thank you. Now, I'm sorry my ball hit you and you fell in the pool. Are you sure you're all right?"

"Fine, no thanks to you." She crossed her arms over her chest. "It's not like this pool is that deep. And I know how to swim. You didn't even have to come over here."

"I guess I felt guilty." He shrugged. "Call it a hero complex or something." He shot her a grin many girls had swooned over.

She simply raised one eyebrow and pursed her lips.

"Katie, are you okay?" Another brunette girl leaned over the side of the pool.

"Who's the hot stud, Katie Belle?" A blonde waved at him from behind the brunette. "Way to start a trip out right!"

When his gaze returned to Katie, her cheeks were much pinker than they'd been before.

"Are you going to put me down or not?" She wiggled again, kicking her legs so high that his hands slipped. "Oof!" She spluttered back to her feet in front of him, shooting him a glare that made him glad looks couldn't kill. "Not what I meant."

"If you hadn't kicked, I could have put you down gracefully." He poked her shoulder. "That one was all on you."

"If you'd left me alone in the first place, I wouldn't even be wet right now." She jabbed him back.

"I already apologized for that. Obviously, you're not gracious enough to forgive and move on." He crossed his arms.

"I'd love to move on, but you're standing in front of the steps."

He glanced over his shoulder and fought back a grimace. So much for being helpful or needed. All he'd succeeded in was making things worse. He moved aside and gestured to the stairs as though presenting her with a new car like a gameshow host.

"Katie." Her brunette friend met her on the top step with a towel. "Girl, that bump looks nasty."

"Well, what do you expect when a stupid volleyball whacked me upside the head?"

"Camden, are you still playing?" Ryan called.

Camden waved his hand and followed Katie and her friend instead. The least he could do was get her some ice and check her for a concussion.

Katie wrapped the towel around her shoulders, hiding the

freckles he was itching to count. "Why on earth did I let you guys talk me into this trip?"

"Because you're my maid of honor and this is what I chose instead of a bachelorette party." The friend steered her to an empty seat.

"And so I get to spend a week being surrounded by clumsy oafs who think they're some sort of Prince Charming?" Katie rubbed her temple.

"The way he looks, he sort of is," the blonde friend chimed in.

"Skye, seriously!"

Camden cleared his throat. All three girls jerked their heads in his direction, each wearing guilty shades of red. "I'll go see if I can find some ice for you. It's the least I can do. And I'd like to take a look at that bump when I get back, if you're okay with that."

He could almost see the protest forming on Katie's lips, but her brunette friend interrupted. "That's a great idea. Thank you so much."

Even three steps away, he could still hear Katie's hiss of a reprimand to her friend. "Bree, it is *not* a good idea! I'm fine."

His lips twitched. Coming on this trip with Ryan had seemed like a reasonable idea when their uncle suggested it. But he hadn't expected to run into anyone so interesting. Especially not on their second day here. Would the girls be staying the whole week too? That could lead to all sorts of fun possibilities.

Now, what would be the best way to come up with an ice pack? Ice machines sat on every floor of the hotel, but he didn't have anything to put ice in. Maybe the little restaurant on the other side of the breezeway would have a baggie or something. He headed toward the smell of fried fish.

"Bree, you know I love you like a sister." Katie shaded her eyes with her hand. "Shoot. Sometimes, I love you more than my sister. But this is a bad way to start a trip I wasn't sure was a good idea in the first place."

"Don't be ridiculous." Skye leaned over the back of the lounge chair, her long blonde hair tickling Katie's bare back. "If you'd just lighten up and have some fun, you'd see that what happened was serendipitous. Not many girls can say they got rescued by a super-hot guy on their first day of vacation."

"Believe it or not, there's more to life than 'super-hot guys.'" Katie's air quotes emphasized her frustration over her friend's flippant attitude.

Skye opened her mouth, but Bree shot her a look that turned her protest into a mere squeak.

Bree patted her hands in front of her, as if calming toddlers. "Okay, I admit this wasn't the best way to start our vacation, but we're here now, and you're okay. Let's just make the best of things and do what we originally planned when we came down here."

"Swim!" Skye dropped her bag by the chair. "And have fun."

"Is that all you think about?" Katie pressed her fingers against the tender spot on the side of her head. "You might as well be hanging out with those idiots in the pool."

"If you insist." Skye flipped her hair over her shoulder and sauntered away.

"You promised to at least try to have fun on this trip." Bree peeled Katie's hand out of the way and studied the bruise.

"I'm sorry. I've never been as good at having fun as Skye." Katie winced as Bree pressed too hard. "I just have a lot on my mind. I mean, as soon as we get back, I'm moving into my new place and starting a new job, all within a week. And then a few weeks after that, you're marrying Nathan, and well ... It's just a lot of change all at once. You know I don't handle change well."

"And that's why we're on this trip. To have one more week to just relax and have fun before we face the real world." Bree bumped shoulders with her. "It may be off to a rough start, but we're in New Orleans. Focus on the good stuff. We get to eat beignets for breakfast."

"I've been dreaming of beignets and café au lait for weeks." Katie let herself give half a smile.

"See? Things are looking better already." Bree squeezed her in a side hug. "Soon your hero will be back with ice and we can get Skye over here to plan everything we want to do over the next few days before we're on to the next stop."

"Hero." Katie sniffed. "More like culprit." Of their own volition her eyes searched the direction he'd walked. Had he really gone to find ice for her, or was that just an excuse to politely escape? Where had he even gone?

Movement inside the restaurant caught her attention. A large, garage-door-style opening at the back was pushed up, allowing diners to spread onto the patio. A bar stood just inside, and Katie could see his spiky, blond hair from here. He leaned up against the bar, chatting with whoever was behind it. The bartender handed over a drink, and her 'hero' accepted it. Katie tore her gaze away. So much for ice.

"Katie?" Bree waved her hand in front of Katie's face.

"Pretty sure I'm not getting that ice pack." Katie pushed against the plastic and stood. The world spun slightly, and she closed her eyes.

"What? Why not?" Bree jumped to her feet and grabbed her elbow.

"I just saw him at the bar of the restaurant over there." Katie took a deep breath to try and stop the dizziness. "He's obviously one of those party boys just here to have a good time."

"Um, Katie." Bree tugged on her arm.

"No, Bree. Just help me to the room, and I'll rig something up myself."

"But Katie."

"What?" Katie huffed and forced her eyes open again. His blue eyes stared back, a look of anger on his face.

"Party boy?" Steel laced his voice.

"Let's just say I don't date guys like you." Katie narrowed her eyes. "I would never date a guy like you."

She started around him, but the world tilted once more.

"You feeling okay?" He thrust a bag of ice into her hands.

"Fine." She gently pressed the cold pack to her temple.

"Really? Because I'm pretty sure you're paler than when I first saw you." He gently cupped her shoulder and pushed her back down in the chair. "Were you dizzy when you stood up?"

"I just got up too fast." She shook her head, unwilling to give in to anything he was saying.

"Mm-hmm." He pulled his cell phone out. "Can you keep your eyes open while I shine a light in them? I want to see if your pupils dilate."

"Oh, really." She tried to push him away and stand again, but Bree joined in his efforts to keep her down.

"Just let him check, Katie."

"How do I know you really are all you claim to be?" Katie winced as the flashlight beam connected with her left eye. "You could have been making that up just to impress me."

"If I were, it obviously didn't work." His lips twitched with noticeable effort to hold back amusement.

It was the first time she'd paid any real attention to his looks, and his five o'clock shadow fascinated her as it shimmered in the afternoon sunshine.

"Oh, here. I got you some water too." He picked up a glass he'd set by her feet and pressed it into her hand.

Water. That was the drink she'd seen him get at the bar. Something innocent. Something for her. Guilt crept up the back of her throat and threatened to choke her.

"Your pupils look good, but you should still probably keep an eye on this bump." He pulled the melting ice away and pressed gently on her tender head. "It doesn't look to be swelling much, but if it does, find an urgent care right away. I'm assuming you're not from around here?"

Katie set her mouth in a line. There was no way he was getting any personal information out of her.

"We're just here for a couple of days." Bree leaned over Katie's shoulder. "I'm Bree."

"Camden." He shook her best friend's hand and shot her a smile. "Sorry I ruined your first night in New Orleans."

"You haven't ruined it. The night is young. We were just relaxing a bit before we head out to find some dinner."

"And music." Skye appeared beside them, dripping on Katie's toes. "I want to dance."

"Maybe we can find somewhere off the main drag that plays jazz." Bree handed Skye a towel. "I heard somewhere that the best stuff isn't on Bourbon Street anymore."

"Oh, come on." Skye flopped beside Katie on the back of the lounge, the vibrations sending a wave of nausea through Katie. "This is New Orleans. We have to at least walk down Bourbon Street."

"I have no desire to get anywhere near that place." Katie shook some condensation off her hand from the melting ice pack. "No way."

"It's basically the same area you said you wanted to go see tomorrow." Bree nudged her shoulder. "Right on the French Quarter."

"But I wanted to see Jackson Square and eat at Café Du Monde. Not walk down the street surrounded by drunks."

"We won't even go into any of the bars, Katie. Just come with us. Bree and I can protect you. I want to soak up the soul of this place." Skye leaned forward.

"Are you sure you're up for something like that?" Camden's voice interrupted their discussion. Katie had honestly forgotten he was there.

"She said she's fine." Skye put a hand on her slender hip. "What are you, a doctor or something?"

"No. But I know enough about medicine to know that was a hard blow." His eyes searched her face, but Katie couldn't tell what he was looking for.

"You should know how hard it was. You're the one who sent it." She tilted the corner of her lips up to ease the words.

"True." That twitch skittered across his mouth again and made her heart skip right along with it.

"I have a great idea!" Skye bounced on the seat, and Katie barely swallowed the groan at the jostle it caused.

"What?"

"Camden and Ryan could come with us. That would make it even safer, and Camden would be there if Katie needs anything for her head."

Katie's eyes flew to Camden's and saw him blink. Was he intrigued or terrified that he'd be cornered into spending the evening with them? Oh, to go back in time and stop Skye from making such a suggestion!

"Who's Ryan?" Bree asked.

"Cam, what's the deal?" Another guy came up behind Camden and put his hand on Camden's shoulder, drawing Katie's attention to Camden's muscled chest. She swallowed and quickly raised her eyes again.

"Ryan, this is Katie and Bree and Skye."

"Oh, yeah. Skye and I met a little while ago in the pool." Ryan's voice sounded on the brink of laughter. "She's invited us to tag along to Bourbon Street tonight. What do you think? Up for it?"

Camden's eyes met Katie's again, but she was frozen, unable to form a coherent thought.

After a moment that seemed eternal, he nodded. "Sure. I could listen to some jazz."

"Aww, man. I just remembered our gas tank is almost empty." Ryan grimaced. "We may have to meet you down there."

"My car's not huge, but I bet we can all squeeze in." Skye shrugged. "It's not like it's that far of a drive."

If Katie didn't kill Skye on this trip, it would be a miracle. How did she get them into such a mess? An evening loomed ahead of her with a man she'd yelled at and possibly hit or kicked during the earlier struggle. Her head throbbed harder than it had a moment before.

"I need some painkillers." For the first time in her life, she was even slightly tempted to look for something even stronger.

A couple of random men jostled Katie's arm as they made their way past her group and on up Bourbon Street. The night was young, the sun barely set, but it was easy to see—and smell—that some people had already been here for hours. Katie attempted to swallow a lump lodged in her throat. Jazz music floated out of almost every building on the road, but it all mixed together in a jumbled cacophony of disjointed sounds, adding to her headache.

"Isn't this amazing?" Skye motioned around them. Her sundress floated against her knees as she swayed to the rhythm of a song.

"Nothing better than this area for some soul pleasing." Ryan linked arms with Skye, and they walked ahead.

"You okay?" Bree wove her arm through Katie's and leaned close. "Is it your head?"

Her head? Yes. But not the way Bree was thinking. The pounding from her bruise was nothing compared to the panic and discomfort building inside her. She squeezed her eyes closed and took a deep breath, hoping to calm her erratic pulse.

"Katie?" Bree pulled her to a stop in the middle of the sidewalk.

Katie forced her eyelids open and focused on her friend's concerned frown. She managed a smile but could tell Bree wasn't buying it. It was the best she could do though.

Why? Why did her body always betray her at times like this?

"You're blocking the path, dummies." A guy in a purple fedora pushed Katie against Bree so he could stomp his way past. The smell of whatever he'd been drinking lingered in the air.

Katie pressed a hand to her mouth, gagging.

"Watch it!" Camden hollered at the man's back. "You girls okay?"

"I'm fine." Bree cut a glance at him and then back at Katie. "Katie's not looking so hot."

"Bree—"

"No, she's right." Camden leaned down and lifted a curl off her forehead to study her bruise. "Are you feeling worse?"

Katie ducked her head. "It's not from earlier." Not earlier today, anyway.

Bree leaned close to catch Katie's words over the noise around them. "Is it … is it from …?"

After glancing at Camden, Katie nodded to her friend.

"Katie, I'm so sorry. I didn't realize this would bring up those memories." Bree squeezed Katie's hands. "Do you need to go? We can find Skye. We might even be able to catch one of those ghost tours she'd mentioned."

"Maybe I should just go back to the hotel. I don't want to ruin your night. No point in all of us suffering just because I can't move on." Katie pulled her hands from Bree's and rubbed her upper arms, despite the heat that lingered in the air. "I'll just call a rideshare or something."

"I don't like the idea of you riding back alone. We said we were going to stick together when we first planned this trip." Bree crossed her arms.

"Skye would hate it if she had to leave now. This is the kind of thing she lives for." Katie motioned the direction Skye had gone. "You stay with her. I'll be fine."

"Do you know where they went?" Camden raised himself on his toes. "I can't even see them anymore."

"I'll call her and ask her to come back so we can come up with a plan." Bree pulled out her phone and quickly dialed their missing friend.

"So, it's not your head?" Camden gave her his full attention the moment Bree turned her back.

"My head is fine. Just a slight headache." She subconsciously rubbed the spot where the ball had hit her.

"Are you sick from something else then?" The frown drew his eyebrows down, leaving a furrow between his eyes that her fingers itched to smooth out.

"It's just ... just something I thought I could handle, but I'm evidently not ready yet." Talk about beating around the bush. But there was no way she was going to pour out her history to someone she'd known only a few hours. Especially after they had such a rocky start.

"She's not answering." Bree held up her phone. "I wonder if it's too loud out here for her to hear it ring."

"Let me try Ryan." Camden grabbed his cell and pressed it to his ear.

Raucous laughter poured from the building nearest them. The neon lights lent an unearthly glow to their surroundings. Katie's heart couldn't decide if it wanted to keep pace with the jazz from this building or the song two doors down. It skittered and spurted until she was sure her toes couldn't possibly be getting enough blood flow. Maybe that was why she suddenly felt wobbly.

"He's going to head them back. Said they're about five pubs ahead of us." Camden turned. "Katie?"

She blinked, and then blinked again, but the earth whirled around her, fuzzing the edges of her vision.

"Katie?" Camden's voice sounded far away. Had he gone to meet Ryan and Skye? But if that were the case, why was he calling her name? Was she supposed to follow him?

Strong arms encircled her as her knees turned to jelly.

---

"Hang in there, Katie." Camden supported the petite brunette for the second time that day, but this time there was no fight in her limp frame.

"Here, Mister. You can use my seat." Behind them, a man pointed to an iron chair on the bar's patio. "Looks like she needs it more than I do."

"Thanks." He easily lifted Katie and moved her out of the crowded path and into the less-crowded pub courtyard. Her head moved as he gently lowered her to the seat.

"Katie." He kept his arms on either side of her until he was sure she wouldn't topple off. "Katie, can you hear me?"

Her hazel eyes blinked once, twice, then stayed open, focusing on him. "What happened?"

"You passed out for a minute."

A look that could only be described as horror crossed her face. "I did?"

"You did," Bree's voice carried over her shoulder. "You're going back to the hotel, whether Skye likes it or not."

"No, Bree. Don't ruin Skye's night over this." Katie buried her face in her hands.

"We'll work something out." Camden gave her upper arm a squeeze, wishing he could do more. This woman, so full of fire and ice earlier in the day, was obviously fighting demons no one else could see. And even though this was the town of witch doctors and voodoo artists, he didn't believe in any of that. Something else haunted her, holding her in a grip too tight to escape. At least without help.

And he wanted more than anything to help. When her hazel eyes had focused on him a moment ago, they changed from terror to trust in an instant. Was there a way to keep that look there, or had he somehow ruined it earlier in the day when she'd declared him a party boy she'd never date?

"What's up with Katie Belle?" Skye's voice broke through his musings.

"She's not feeling well." Bree tugged on Camden's sleeve and pulled him up. "We've got to get her away from this atmosphere."

"Atmosphere?" He glanced around. "You mean the crowds?"

"More like the type of people making up the crowds." Bree's mouth pinched closed as if she were forcibly keeping the rest of the story from slipping out.

Camden shook his head in confusion.

"Look." Bree glanced over her shoulder at Katie to make sure their conversation wasn't overheard before turning her attention back to him. "It's not my story to tell, okay? But let's just suffice it to say that Katie has had some really bad history with alcoholics."

A dim light went on in Camden's head. Not enough to show him the full picture but enough to explain at least partly why Katie had panicked earlier. The whicker of a horse drew his attention to the road.

"I have an idea."

Bree looked over at the carriage and then back at him, a smile crossing her face. "Perfect. Now, we just have to convince her."

"This isn't going to be easy, is it?" Camden studied the fascinating woman sitting nearby, looking worse by the minute as Skye hovered at her side.

"You got that right, buster." Bree thumbed over her shoulder. "You go see if you can catch one of those, and I'll try and convince her this is a great plan."

Several carriages passed before Camden found an empty one. From the looks of things behind him, though, that was probably just as well. Katie looked like she was adamantly refusing.

"I don't even know this guy, and you're suggesting I go off on a carriage ride with him in a strange city." Nervous energy laced Katie's voice.

"I have that app on my phone that lets me see where you are, remember?" Bree waved her cell. "I'll check it every few minutes to make sure you're still riding up and down the area at the speed of a carriage, and we'll meet you guys back at the car in an hour. This way, none of us has to give up having fun this evening."

Katie's eyes were wide as Bree pushed her toward Camden. He raised an eyebrow and held out his hand, willing her to accept and come with him. Not only because he wanted to get her out of this toxic environment but also because he was looking forward to hopefully breaking through that shell she'd built around herself. Maybe even convince her he wasn't as bad as she thought.

"You coming, lady?" The carriage driver gave her a dirty

look. "I don't plan to sit here all night. And if you've been drinking too much and are needing a ride, I'd rather you call someone else. I don't want sick in the back of my carriage."

Katie's face paled in the neon lights.

Camden quickly reached out and grabbed her hand, giving a little tug. "She hasn't had a thing to drink tonight except water and coffee. We're getting in."

"Relax, Katie. You're going to have so much fun." Bree waved at them from the curb as the carriage pulled out into the foot traffic, meandering slowly up the street amid the pedestrians.

"Where all does this ride take us?" Katie studied her hands instead of their surroundings.

"I talked him into doing his usual route through the French Quarter and then a little side trip to go straight to our parking lot, so we won't have to walk through any of that again." Camden pointed his thumb in the direction of the Bourbon Street noise. "I've heard the French Quarter is beautiful in the moonlight."

"With all that amazing architecture, it's beautiful no matter when." Her back straightened a bit. "But the colors obviously stand out more in the daytime."

A tour group on Segways passed them on the sidewalk, the guide spewing some story about ghosts of former people who had occupied the buildings they drove past. Soft, mellow blues music wafted from a restaurant and wrapped its fingers around them. People strolled the streets. Lit balconies full of people and plants decorated the sides of many buildings.

"I'm sorry you had to leave. I really would've been fine just taking a taxi or something." Katie picked at an invisible spot on her capris.

He covered her hand with his and gave a squeeze. "I wasn't

really interested in Bourbon Street either. I'm just hanging out with Ryan this week."

Slipping her fingers back out of his, she tucked them under her thighs. "Still. It's not fun to end up being the babysitter."

He leaned as close as he dared. "You're definitely not a baby. You're a beautiful woman. And I don't feel like I'm forced to watch you."

She swallowed so hard he could see the muscles of her throat work.

"Is this your first time in New Orleans?" Maybe a change of subject would lighten the mood.

"Second." She stared in the direction of her side of the carriage. "My family visited here when I was a teenager. My uncle took us out to several plantations, but I don't think I'll be able to talk the girls into doing something like that tomorrow. Too much history and not enough fun."

"Maybe later this week." He leaned back in the seat, draping his arm across the back as casually as possible.

"We leave Wednesday morning." She glanced back at him.

"Too bad. We're supposed to be here until Saturday. At least that's what Ryan told Uncle John. And since Uncle John is footing the bill, I'm figuring we'll stick fairly close to that plan so we don't get cut off."

"Must be nice to have someone foot the bill for you to have fun." She leaned back and closed her eyes, not seeming to notice that her hair rested on his forearm.

"In some ways. In other ways, I think Uncle John was hoping I'd be a good influence on Ryan and keep him out of trouble."

One of Katie's eyes opened again and studied him. "He's the troublemaker? I thought that was you."

Camden chuckled. "He's the one who doesn't take things as seriously. Let's just leave it at that."

"Sounds like Skye." Katie shook her head, her curls tickling his skin. "No wonder those two hit it off. Maybe it's a good thing we'll only be here one more day. Who knows what kind of trouble they might've gotten into?"

The horse clip-clopped on, but they settled into a comfortable silence. He inched just slightly closer, and her eyes popped open once more. Time stood still for several seconds as their gazes remained locked. Was her heart beating as hard as his right now?

The carriage hit a bump and jostled them. She landed pressed to his side. His arm slid down off the back of the bench and held her there for a split second before letting go. What was he doing? She'd just admitted they'd be here only one more day. What was the point of pursuing anything with this girl who did crazy things to his heart?

She straightened again. "I think I recognize some of these buildings. We must be getting close to the parking lot."

He nodded.

"I know I haven't shown much appreciation today, but I wanted to say thanks for finding a way to get me off of that street." Katie studied her hands again.

"My pleasure."

The carriage halted, and Camden paid the man before helping Katie down. The streetlights illuminated the rows of cars still filling the lot. As they neared Skye's convertible, Bree waved.

"Well, hey, lovebirds!" Ryan laughed as if he'd told the funniest joke ever.

Katie stepped a bit farther away from Camden, and he missed her nearness immediately.

"Was it so much fun?" Bree climbed in the backseat and pulled Katie in beside her. "I've always wanted to go on one of those rides."

"You could've come with us." Katie scooted closer to Bree as Camden climbed in beside her, although their knees still pressed against each other. There wasn't quite enough room for three people their size in the backseat of a car designed more for looks than anything.

"That bench didn't look big enough. Maybe I can talk Nathan into taking me on one on our honeymoon. I know for a fact they have them in New York City too."

"So, you're for sure going to the Big Apple for your honeymoon?" Skye turned with interest while stopped at a red light.

"Nathan won't answer me outright, but he hasn't denied it. And that's the location I gave the most hints about." Bree shook her head. "He keeps saying he wants to surprise me."

"I'd hate that. No idea what to pack if you don't know where you're going." Skye flipped a strand of hair over her shoulder.

"I don't really care where we go as long as Nathan's there."

"I want a guy like that one day. One who makes any location better by simply being there." Had Katie just cut her eyes his way?

They'd only just met and would probably never see each other again after tonight. Besides, lifelong romances didn't start with a volleyball to the head.

Back at the hotel, Camden helped the girls out of the backseat. "It was great hanging out with you this evening."

"Thanks again for the carriage ride." Katie's reply came out almost a whisper. "And everything."

"You're welcome." He caught the tips of her fingers as she passed and gave them a small tug.

Would he get to spend any more time with her before they left? He should've gotten her number or something. She intrigued him more than anyone he'd ever met.

"Coming, Cam?" Ryan waved the door key.

"Yeah." Camden followed his cousin down the hallway in the opposite direction the girls had gone. "I'm beat."

"Well, you better rest up tonight, then, because I have a great plan. You're going to love it."

Why did those words leave dread sifting through Camden's heart instead of excitement? Ryan's plans almost never ended well. What on earth had he come up with now?

"This is a bad idea." Camden ran a hand through his short hair and studied the crowds milling around the famous green awning the next morning.

"It's not." Ryan bounced on his toes as they waited for the light to change. "Why would Skye have told me where they were going if she didn't intend for us to join them?"

"And how do you plan to find them in this crowd?" Camden reluctantly followed Ryan across the street, the smell of coffee and sugar drawing him more than his resolve to watch over his cousin.

"There." Ryan pointed to three now-familiar heads around a table on the patio. He held up his phone. "Skye texted me."

Evidently, Skye really had meant for them to join the girls this morning. Camden still had his doubts. Skipping the line and main entrance, Ryan dashed up to the metal railing instead and leaned over.

"Hey, gorgeous girls."

Skye squealed with laughter, her coffee sloshing danger-ously as she rocked back in her chair. Katie, on the other hand, choked on her beignet. She pressed a napkin to her lips and fanned her face as the coughs continued despite several hard pats on the back from Bree.

"Fancy seeing you here, guys." Bree shot a look at Skye and then at Ryan. "Are you coming around to join us?"

The look Katie shot him before he turned was somewhere between mortification and murder. Why hadn't he tried to talk Ryan into something else? Even one of those stupid vampire tours would be better than the deadly looks sure to come his way all through breakfast. Although by the smells radiating throughout the place, those glares wouldn't hamper his appetite.

"I don't see any extra chairs around." Skye half stood and then sat again as he and Ryan approached the girls' table. "Do you think we could steal one from inside?"

"I'm sure they need those chairs in there, Skye." Katie's voice was icy.

"Well, maybe you can just share with me, then, Ryan." Skye shot a saucy grin at Camden's cousin and patted the edge of her seat.

"I'll just lean against the rail." Camden surveyed Skye's side of the table, but the way the chair had to be positioned to hold both her and Ryan, there was no way he could squeeze by without climbing over someone's lap. He spun and avoided Katie's eyes as he slid past her and sat behind Bree.

"What can I get you boys?" A waitress with a black bowtie and white paper hat stood at their table, one eyebrow raised slightly higher than the other, as if to reprimand them for trying to fit too many people in such a small space.

"An order of beignets and a café au lait, please." Camden gave her a grin he hoped included some apology too.

"Same for me. Anyone else need anything?" Ryan acted as if

intruding on someone else's breakfast were the most natural thing in the world.

"It's a small world, huh?" Bree took a sip from her mug.

"Come on. This is New Orleans! We had to come here at least once." Ryan snickered with Skye.

"And it just happened to be the same morning we're here?" Katie pursed her lips. How did she get them to look that small when they were so plump and inviting when she relaxed?

"Oh, come off it, Katie." Skye picked up the powdered sugar shaker and gave her beignets another coating. "Won't it be fun to hang out together today? After all, we're leaving tomorrow."

"Where are you going next?" Camden gratefully accepted a mug of chicory-laced coffee from the waitress.

"The beach." Katie's words cut off Skye's potential response, and the blonde didn't look too happy about it. "We're spending a night on the Gulf Coast. Skye thinks she needs to work on her tan."

"How else am I going to look good in my bridesmaid dress in a month?" Skye held out an arm that already had a healthy glow.

"You're not supposed to be the focus. Everyone's going to admire Bree because it's her wedding." Katie leaned back in her seat and crossed her legs.

"Well, since I'm the one who will be in white, I could definitely use some work on my tan. Those last few weeks of school didn't give me much time out of class or the library." Bree finished off the last bite of her beignets and licked her fingertips. "Although I probably don't need to eat many more of these either, or I'll need another fitting."

"Please." Katie playfully bumped her friend's shoulder. "As skinny as you are?"

"The beach will be relaxing anyway. Nice to have a few

days to just soak up the salt water and sun." Bree cradled her mug in her hands. "I wish Nathan could have come, though."

"That would sort of defeat the purpose of a girls' trip, wouldn't it?" Katie shot a look at Skye but was completely ignored.

"You girls playing the tourist today?" Camden hoped a change of subject might ease the discord.

"Why? You guys planning to follow us all day?"

Instead, his question just earned him the position of being on Katie's bad side.

"We don't have any plans. When I suggested we come down here, we sort of figured we'd play it by ear." Ryan dusted sugar off his fingers. "I bet you scoped out all the tourist websites and made a list, ranked by which building you wanted to visit most."

"I didn't." Skye laughed and flipped her hair over her shoulder. "I suggested the city, but Bree and Katie are the planners. I said we should just wing it like you, and you should have seen their faces."

"We'll be wandering around the French Quarter and Jackson Square this morning." Bree placed her empty cup on the table. "Y'all are more than welcome to join us."

Katie's look said otherwise.

"Sounds great." Ryan seemed intent on ignoring anything but what he wanted to see and hear. "Are we ready?"

Bills paid, Camden followed the rest of the group out of the busy café and onto the street already teeming with tourists. Bree and Katie led the way past stores opening for the day, restaurants with chalkboards declaring various specials, and vendors arranging their wares along the roads and alleys. The Cathedral's spires filled the sky on one side of the famous square, and the girls in front paused to stare for a few seconds.

He couldn't blame them. The architecture and history of

this city begged to be admired and appreciated. Ryan bumped into him from behind.

"Sorry, Cam. Didn't realize we had stopped." Ryan leaned around Camden's shoulders and glanced at their surroundings. "What gives? There's no streetlight holding us up."

"I think the girls are deciding what to do first."

"Who's the dude on the horse?" Ryan pointed to the center of the square.

"Andrew Jackson." Katie rolled her eyes. "You know … the guy the square is named after?"

"Huh."

As they made their way around, Skye and Bree showed more interest in shopping while Katie kept getting distracted by the plaques about history. She wandered into the doorway of a museum, but Skye refused to go, so Katie stepped back out, shoulders bowed. Street artists lined the sidewalks, showing off their work. A caricature vendor caught Skye's eye.

"Oh, let's have him do ours." She bounced on her toes. "Wouldn't it be fun to have this memory in ink?"

"He uses chalk." Katie pointed out. "And who would keep the drawing? It's not like we can have him do five so we can all have one."

"Skye's right." Bree tugged Katie's arm. "Let's do this. Maybe just the girls, though. To commemorate our last trip together."

"I'm doing this for you, Bree." Katie perched on the stool.

Camden smiled as Bree said something to Katie that made her grin. Had he seen a real smile on her face before? He'd caught expressions of anger, frustration, fear, and pain, but a smile practically made her glow. What would it be like if she ever shot a look like that his way?

"Now let's do one with the boys too." Skye scooted over and waved at Camden and Ryan to join them.

Camden knew Ryan would want the spot by Skye, so he took the other spot, behind and between Katie and Bree. Katie's back was stiff and straight, as if afraid she might touch him if she relaxed. Ryan paused to talk about something with the artist before he meandered over to their group.

"Ready?" The artist called, winking at them.

Ryan snickered while the rest of their party nodded agreements. Having someone draw him gave Camden a strange sensation. Even as a comic-style character, to know a person was studying him intently enough to capture his various traits and maybe even some personality on paper seemed intimate. In less time than Camden expected, the artist nodded that he was finished.

When Skye saw the finished product, she roared with laughter. "Oh, perfect!"

Katie and Bree gasped about the same time. Camden braced himself and looked. The paper showed only Katie and him, pink hearts fluttering around them as they smiled at each other in chalk.

Before he could react, Katie stormed away from their group. This had to be Ryan's idea. No one else would have suggested it. Bree chased after her friend while Skye and Ryan settled the bill and gathered their rolled-up artwork.

Although Camden didn't mind the idea behind the drawing, he couldn't understand why Ryan would do such a thing. It's not like he and Katie would have time to get to know each other and actually form a relationship. The girls left tomorrow, and there was no way Katie would give him her cell number to try and do anything long distance. He followed the rest of the group to where Katie studied another plaque.

"The Louisiana Purchase was made just over there." Katie pointed. "Can you feel the history surrounding us right now? So much has happened in this area."

Evidently, she was going to pretend the drawing had never happened.

"Ugh. If I wanted a history lesson, I'd have taken more classes." Skye turned on her heel. "See the statues in each corner? They're the four seasons. Let's do fun selfies with them."

"What's the point of coming to places like this if you never soak up the history of it?" Katie shrugged. "Life can't be all about shopping and having fun."

"What do you do again?" Camden couldn't fight the intrigue anymore.

"She's a librarian." Bree squeezed her friend's arm.

"For a school?"

"No. For a public library." Katie folded her arms across her chest as if to challenge him should he think the job was dorky. He didn't.

"I bet that's really interesting." He stuck his hands in his pockets. "I always stop right inside the doors of the one back home and just breathe for a moment. Nothing like the smell of books."

---

Who was this guy? They'd definitely gotten off to a rocky start, and Katie had planned to keep it that way, but then he went and said things like that, setting her heart reaching toward his. Ridiculous. After today she'd never see him again. She wasn't the kind of girl who went for vacation flings. Steadiness and permanence were all she wanted.

"Isn't the river just over there?" Ryan pointed toward the levee on the other side of the square. "What if we grab some sandwiches and go picnic on the riverside?"

"I love that idea." Skye flashed him a beaming smile.

Of course, she did. Skye seemed to like all of Ryan's suggestions. Otherwise, he wouldn't even be here right now. Still ... a sandwich and a view of the water did sound nice.

"If I remember correctly, there's a restaurant just over that way. They're supposed to have amazing po' boys." Bree pointed south. "It's even on the way to the park."

"Sounds good." Camden patted his flat stomach. "I could definitely go for some shrimp."

How did he stay so fit? She'd seen his toned arms and chest yesterday at the pool. Was he still lifeguarding somewhere? Surely a physical therapist didn't get that much of a workout in his day-to-day routine. She refused to ask, though. For one thing, she didn't want to let on that she'd noticed something so personal. And for another, she didn't want to encourage anyone to continue pushing them together into a relationship that would never have a chance.

The line was out the door of the restaurant Bree wanted to try, but since they weren't in a hurry, everyone agreed to wait. The smells coming from inside advertised it would be worth it. Katie fixed her attention on the small paper menu that Bree had plucked from a holder near the door. Everything sounded amazing.

"Brave enough to try crawfish?" Camden's voice pulled her from her decision making.

She wrinkled her nose. "No. I've heard it's good, but I can't even stand the thought of eating a lobster. They're just so ugly. And I especially can't get past the thought of what they eat before we eat them."

"So, no desire to go up to the northeast and indulge in lobster brought in fresh that day?" He leaned against the door-jamb. "I've always thought it would be fun to explore Maine and do something like that."

"I've always wanted to see Maine too." She twisted the

paper in her hands. "I don't know. It'd have to be something special for me to try it even then though. But lobsters do sound more appetizing than crawfish."

"So, you're not from Maine, then."

Oops. That eliminated at least one state in the list of possible places she lived. "No. Not from Maine."

"I didn't think so."

"What? Why?"

"Your accent." Camden winked. "It pretty much assures me you're from the South. I just haven't quite figured out which part yet." The end of his statement was almost a question, but she wasn't about to answer.

They moved forward with the crowd, and Katie closed her eyes to enjoy the air conditioning blowing directly on her from the vent by the door. A body pressed against hers and her eyes flew open. Camden took a step back again.

"Sorry." He pointed at some people leaving. "They were rather aggressive as they pushed by."

But his face didn't look completely sorry despite his apology. Instead, he appeared to have enjoyed it as much as she had. Another thing never to admit.

Sandwiches procured, their group strolled down the Moonwalk, surveying the park for a good place to eat. They settled on a spot near a shade tree. Steamers rolled up and down the river below them, occasionally sounding their horns. Katie took a bite of her lunch and let her imagination follow the current on down toward the Gulf. She was surrounded by history, but none of her group seemed to care.

When she agreed to come on this trip, she knew it was going to be more about the fun than anything else, but she'd hoped to set foot inside at least one museum. With the inclusion of the boys, there was even less of a chance. At least tomorrow they'd leave the guys behind, and she could relax a bit more.

A sharp pinch to her toe brought her out of her reverie. "Ouch!"

She brushed against her foot, knocking off several bugs.

"Fire ants." Camden's hand grabbed her lower leg and moved her away from the dirt mound she hadn't noticed. A thrill shot up her body, despite the lack of romance in the touch.

Where had that come from? She hadn't felt anything like that when he held her in the pool yesterday—not beyond humiliation and pain. Or last night in the carriage. Maybe it was triggered by the ant bites.

"I think we got them all." Camden's fingers trailed her shins, turning her ankles over to check underneath.

She jerked her legs away and tucked them close to her body. "Thanks. I didn't even notice them when we first sat down."

"The food probably attracted them." Camden gathered his trash and stood, not fazed at all by what had just happened.

Was she so repulsive? She crumbled the rest of her chips and added them to her Styrofoam container. Could she seem any more incompetent? First, she got knocked into the pool by a stupid volleyball, then passed out because of her ridiculous ghosts, and now she couldn't even watch out for ants before taking a seat. Even if they had a chance to see each other beyond today, he probably wouldn't want to take it.

"Let's go shopping." Skye jumped up and threw her garbage away. "There's a mall over there. All air conditioned. My father wanted me to bring him back some hot sauce."

"I thought we'd talked about going to see a plantation nearby." Katie brushed her capris off.

"Oh, Katie. That's so depressing." Skye pouted. "All that talk of slave labor, no air conditioning, and women forced to wear corsets and hoop skirts. Bleh. I might as well go take a nap."

Skye might think a plantation was boring, but Katie considered shopping just as dull. What had happened to all the plans she and Bree had made for this road trip? Wasn't Bree the one to decide? She was the bride, after all. Both girls looked to their friend, who appeared torn and distressed.

Katie sighed. There would be no history for her on this trip. She'd have to come back another time by herself. Skye was too influential to overcome.

"Come on. You said something about wanting to buy bridesmaids' gifts along the way." Katie looped her arm through Bree's. "Onward to the mall."

Would the guys abandon them for such a girly activity? But they followed along, flanking Skye. She giggled and pointed as they meandered farther south down the Moonwalk and past the casino and aquarium. The river held most of Katie's attention, though.

"Look. There's a ferry that takes you across the water." Katie pointed.

"It would be more fun to ride on one of those big paddleboats." Skye giggled.

"True. But until I start getting paid, I'm trying to conserve as much money as possible, and a ride on one of those is not in my budget this trip." Katie raised an eyebrow at her friend. "A free ferry ride on the other hand ..."

"Maybe we can catch one on the way back up. We're parked up closer to Jackson Square, so we'll have to come back this way anyway." Bree tugged on Katie's arm.

"Sounds good to me." Camden's voice carried from behind her.

"It's only a five-minute ride across. It's not like it's going to be that thrilling." Skye's tone held a touch of disbelief.

"But for five minutes, we can pretend we're Tom Sawyer." Camden came up even with Katie and Bree and shot them a wink.

How had he known that was exactly what she'd been thinking? To live out a few moments of Mark Twain's imagination would be a dream come true. Was this guy for real? Had she finally found someone she could be interested in, only to have to leave him tomorrow?

# 4

What was going through her head? Camden studied Katie as she obviously forced herself to pass the dock to the ferry and headed toward the shopping mall. She hadn't looked happy all day. Was there more to it than Ryan and him tagging along on their girls' trip? She'd visibly slumped when they nixed her idea of going through a museum or plantation. But neither of her friends had noticed, so maybe he was reading too much into it.

The air conditioning chilled his skin as they stepped through the mall doors. Places like this intimidated him. Despite studying the maps of layouts, he always got turned around and ended up in the opposite direction from where he thought he was heading.

"What all are we looking for?" Bree led their group to one of the directories. "They have several little shops that are more New Orleans things instead of just regular name-brand outlet stores. Here's one that's Mardi Gras themed."

"Ooh. Let's go there. We could all buy a mask!" Skye

followed the instructions on the map to figure out where the shop was located.

"There's a little Café du Monde on the third floor in the food court." He glanced over all the shoulders in front of him. "We could get some coffee for a pick-me-up."

"Mm." Katie let out a deep sigh. "Coffee sounds amazing right now."

"We have to go this direction to get to the store Skye wanted to see. Let's start that way, and we'll work our way around and then get you guys some caffeine." Bree pointed to their right and then headed off without waiting for anyone to agree or protest.

Bree was fairly good at keeping the peace. Camden would give her that. But something told him that, more often than not, her peacekeeping worked only so far as Katie acquiesced and let Skye have her way. He ended up next to the petite brunette at the back of their group as they wove through the crowds.

Would she have another panic attack being surrounded by so many people? But there was no sign of distress about her today. What had Bree whispered? Something about alcohol?

"Did you want to shop for something?" Katie followed her friends through the door of a store full of feathered masks, beads, and other paraphernalia related to Mardi Gras. She picked up a bag of beignet mix and then set it back down.

"I'm sort of just along for the ride this week."

A short laugh escaped her mouth. "I know the feeling."

"You didn't want to come on your girls' trip?" He fingered a pack of beads and then set them aside.

"This is our sixth road trip together. The other ones weren't quite this ... well, complicated for lack of a better word." Katie flipped through a rack of T-shirts with various New Orleans logos.

"Complicated?"

"With this many stops." She looked into his eyes for the first time since the caricature fiasco. "In college, we loaded up and took a trip to the beach for Spring Break one year. And to the Smokies another. This one, I think we added too much to it. It might've been better if we'd done what you guys planned to do. Just stay here all week."

"Then you could have done some things you wanted to do too."

Her eyes widened for a moment, and then she looked away. "I'll come back someday. I know I appreciate history more than Skye does. And Bree just wants to make everyone happy."

"Katie! Look at these!" Skye waved from the other side of the store, where several racks of masks hung.

He could have sworn he heard Katie mutter "Duty calls" as she moved past him and headed over to see what the other girls had found.

Ryan had donned a mask that was half yellow and half green. Camden would never tell him, but it made his cousin look rather sickly. On top of his head, Ryan wore a cheap top hat, complete with gaudy feathers.

"Wouldn't it be fun if we all wore one to the rehearsal?" Skye held a blue and green feathered number over her face. The colors set her blue eyes blazing as she beamed underneath.

"What about Cora?" Katie leaned against another rack and crossed her arms over her chest.

"I thought we'd just pick one out to take her. My sister's not terribly picky." Bree peeked out from behind a mirror.

"So, you're on board with this idea?" Katie frowned just enough to put a slight wrinkle in her forehead. "I mean, this is your rehearsal. Not Skye's."

"I know it is. But why not? We don't have to be serious at the rehearsal. It's not the actual wedding." Bree slid a white mask with silver and gold accents over her face. "And it's sort of fun."

"And Nathan will be okay with it?" Katie looked more uncomfortable with each passing moment. Once again, Cam wondered what she was thinking.

"Tell you what. If he doesn't want us to, we won't." Bree held her mask up and gave Katie a look that could only be described as puppy dog eyes. "But won't it be fun to have them as a memory of our last girls' trip together?"

Katie blinked a couple times, pinched her lips together, and sighed. "Sure, Bree."

"Ooh, yay! Your favorite color is purple, right? There are tons of purple masks, since it's one of the Mardi Gras colors." Bree ran her hands down a collection of masks that Camden would never have picked for Katie. He hadn't known her long, but Katie was not the type who would wear something so garish.

"I'm not sure I'm a feather kind of girl." Katie looked around, as if hoping to escape or have a miracle drop from the sky.

Camden studied the masks around them too. There. On the far wall, several glittery masks adorned with only a few swirls of color and some pearls hung in rows. He stepped around another display and pulled off one with three different shades of purple. It was simple, yet elegant.

"How about this?" He cradled it in his hands so that only Katie could see it.

Her eyes lit up and she slowly reached for it. With a tug of the elastic, it fit over her curls and her hazel eyes, showing only a shadow of the spunk he'd seen in her the day before. And yet, it also was like a frame on a work of art, magnifying the beauty already there.

"Perfect!" Bree's breathless squeal stole Katie's gaze from him

But he'd seen the appreciation written there. And maybe something else? He swallowed the disappointment in the small connection being broken.

"Time for coffee?" Camden motioned toward the cash register.

Purchases made, they found their way up to the smaller café and ordered coffee and beignets. Skye and Bree ran off to check out "one more store" that Skye just couldn't pass up, but Katie leaned back in the plastic chair in the food court and savored her afternoon treat. She propped her feet on the seat across from her and sighed after a sip of her drink.

"How are your bites?" Camden leaned over to look at her ankles.

"I hadn't even thought of them again until now." She opened her eyes. "I guess they itch a bit, but I'll live. I'm not allergic to them or anything."

"I'm sorry you've had such a rough experience here. This city has some amazing things to offer." He licked powdered sugar off his fingers.

"It hasn't been all bad. Just ... not exactly what I planned." She studied the top of her cup. "I guess after tonight, anything that happens to me for the rest of the trip I'll have to deal with myself. You won't be around to whisk me off in a carriage or scoop me out of the water."

Ryan jumped up and collected his trash. "I'm going to see if I can catch up to the others."

"That was abrupt." Katie stood too.

"Yeah." Camden walked with her to the trash bin. "I wish I could get a better read on him, but Ryan has been acting a little crazier than ever this trip. Probably why my Uncle John wanted me to tag along. I'm supposed to be keeping him away from trouble."

"Good luck." Katie swung her bag with the mask between them as they walked.

"Thanks. I probably need it."

The others came out of the store as he and Katie arrived, so they walked toward the entrance. They finally arrived after Skye came across two more stores that she 'just had to stop at for a minute.' The only other purchase Katie made was a package of pralines. The afternoon sun hung low in the sky as they exited back into the muggy outside.

"On to the ferry?" Katie's feet pointed north.

"You weren't serious about that, were you?" Skye lugged five or six bags now and looked as though she'd had enough walking for the day.

"It's only a few minutes. Come on, Skye. We did what you wanted." Katie tugged on her friend's arm.

"Fine." Skye slumped along behind Katie and Bree, her shoulders sagging and her feet dragging much more than they had that morning. Was it because she was tired or because she was being led to do something she didn't desire?

They arrived at the dock just in time to make the ferry leaving without waiting half an hour. Out on the water, the wind lifted some of the air's heaviness and cooled things off a bit. He leaned against the railing next to Katie and watched emotions fly across her face. Was she doing as they'd discussed earlier and imagining herself in Mark Twain's story?

<hr>

Katie couldn't help it. She relished her small victory. Skye might be sitting on one of the benches, loaded under bags of new purchases they didn't have room for in their already laden trunk, but Katie's heart practically bubbled like the water rushing out behind the ferry as it made its way across the churning Mississippi.

Next to her, Camden leaned against the rail, and she was aware of exactly how far apart they stood. Sometime today, she'd gone from anger at his presence to almost craving it. Not that she could do anything about it, except enjoy these few moments in their small amount of time left together.

Then, she could put this fairy tale behind her and focus once again on her real life. Vacations made it too easy to play pretend and give in to wishful thinking. Just five more days and then this road trip would end, and she wouldn't have to struggle with such things anymore.

The ride was short. Only a few minutes across and then a few minutes back. But to see the strong, muddy waters all around her, to smell the salt of the delta, to touch a piece of America that formed so much of its history—all of that made the ride so much more.

Bree leaned against her other side and smiled over at her. "I'm glad you talked us into this. It was neat to ride a ferry."

"You'll probably take one on your honeymoon. Maybe out to Ellis Island." Katie scrunched her nose.

"But you won't be there." Bree laid her head on Katie's shoulder. "And that makes me a little sad. Not enough to invite you along, mind you. I guess I'm just feeling a little bittersweet on this trip."

"Me too." Katie's voice came out rougher than she'd intended.

Their group walked back through the French Quarter toward the parking garage where they'd started their morning. The street artists packed up and gathered easels and chalk, pedestrians scurried toward restaurants or parking lots. A quiet settled over the area in this late afternoon before the evening festivities would pick up.

"Care to have your fortune read?" A woman's voice from a side street called to them.

"Oh!" Skye's energy level spiked a bit. "What fun! Look. She reads palms."

"Skye, you can't seriously believe all that stuff." Katie put her hands on her hips. "There's no science to it. It's basically a bunch of old wives' tales, and there are tons of different websites that tell you just the opposite of what another says."

"Everything I think is fun on this trip, you turn your nose up at." Skye huffed. "What's it going to hurt to let her look at my hand?"

"I can see you don't believe." The woman stepped forward from the small table she'd been packing up. "Let me give you a sample."

Before Katie could protest, the woman grabbed Katie's left hand between her own slightly wrinkled fingers, gnarled as though in the beginning stages of arthritis. Katie tugged, but the woman's grip was strong. Skye laughed as if this were the best joke of the day, and that was saying something considering what they'd pulled earlier with the caricature artist.

"Now, this is your weaker hand. Most people believe that means this is the hand that shows more of the future than the past." The woman's red nail trailed the line down the middle of Katie's hand. "Here's your head line. Very straight. You're a very realistic thinker, yes?"

"Pretty sure I just proved that by saying all of this was a bunch of boloney." Katie's mutter caused Camden to snicker behind her.

"Here's your life line." The woman didn't seem to mind

Katie's snark. "It's straight. That means you don't trust others easily. But see all these breaks in your lines? Something very traumatic has happened to you."

Katie swallowed a lump of fear. How could the lady know that simply from her hand? Did her fear and brokenness show through her palms? She darted a glance over her shoulder, but no one else seemed to think anything of what the woman had spoken.

"No fate line. That means you make your own destiny." The woman smiled up at Katie.

"What about romance?" Skye leaned over as if she could see what the woman saw. "Does it say anything about a romance blossoming?"

Ryan chuckled from her other side.

The woman scooted her finger over towards Katie's pinky. "The marriage line. It's strong, and just one. That usually means one romance for life. And it's fairly far down from your finger. So, not too late in life. Possibly soon."

Katie jerked her hand away with enough force to free herself from the woman's grasp. She spun on her heel and marched toward the car, not caring if the others followed or not. Skye and all her romantic notions were getting to Katie. The week couldn't end soon enough. Then she could be free from her flighty friend for several weeks until Bree's wedding.

"Katie!" Bree panted as she caught up to her. "Wait, Katie. You said it yourself. It's just something silly. She doesn't really know what's going to happen in your life."

"I don't believe any of it. I'm just tired of Skye trying to shove me into something I don't want." Katie motioned over her shoulder to where their friend stood, getting her own palm read now.

"Please don't be mad." Bree tugged on her arm.

"You know I can't stay mad at you."

The others caught up a few minutes later, all solemn and quiet. Maybe Skye's ridiculous future predictions had been bleaker than Katie's? Or just included something Skye didn't want to hear?

"We should probably go get dinner on the way back, huh?" Katie switched her shopping bag to her other hand, trying to put from her mind all the palmist had told her. She really didn't believe it, but all the talk of romance during the day was starting to get to her.

"Ugh. I'm thinking I might just grab something at that little restaurant next to our hotel and eat in the room." Bree stifled a yawn. "Nathan wanted to video chat this evening."

"Ryan and I had talked about coming back down here to do one of those ghost tours." Skye shook one of her legs. "But I want to change shoes first."

"Oh." Katie swallowed some disappointment. So much for making the most of the last night in this city.

"You're more than welcome to join us." Skye lifted a shoulder. "I just didn't think it was something you were interested in."

"I'm not. It's fine." Katie stored her purchases in the back and slid into the backseat of Skye's convertible.

"My uncle recommended a Cajun restaurant just down the street from our hotel, and I haven't had a chance to try it out yet." Camden leaned against the side of the car. "If you're up for a short walk when we get back, I'd love the company."

Katie pulled her bottom lip between her teeth. Should she? She still didn't really know him despite having spent a day and a half together. And yet ... an evening in the room listening to Bree gush to her fiancé didn't sound great either.

"Do it." Bree's whisper carried from the front seat.

"I'll chip in for dessert." One corner of Camden's mouth rose.

"Okay. See you back at the motel."

Had she made a mistake? But hadn't she also wanted to spend more time with him while she could? This was her opportunity to live this fantasy just a bit longer. And Bree was only a text away.

Camden was waiting by the pool when Katie came down from stashing her bags in the girls' room. The evening sunlight cast a golden glow over everything, and the water sparkled behind him, highlighting his spiky blonde hair. His mouth lifted in a grin, and she had to will her heartbeat back to a normal rhythm.

"Hey." He met her at the bottom of the stairs. "You look nice."

"It's just a sundress." Though she was glad she'd changed into it.

"Well, it still looks nice on you." He motioned toward the street. "Want to walk or take my car?"

"Now that the sun's lower, it's not as hot. A walk might be nice." She hitched her purse strap a little higher on her shoulder.

"It's not far, according to the map on my phone. We'll see how my navigating skills do." He led the way out of the court-yard and onto the sidewalk.

Silence hung between them, but it wasn't awkward or

stilted. Instead, it was comfortable, as though both relished the time away from their chatty friends. His navigating skills proved reliable because a few minutes later, he pointed her toward an eatery. A dark red awning shaded the door and scrolled ironwork adorned the second-floor windows.

"Do you like Cajun food?" He sat across from her at the cloth-covered table and handed her a menu.

"I don't know that I've ever had any authentic Cajun. Just whatever the restaurants serve north of here. Or what you can buy in a box." She ran her finger down the options, searching through various prices before looking at the actual meals. This place was more expensive than she was used to.

Camden pulled her menu down and pointed to a listing on the opposite page from where she'd been looking. A sampler platter with étouffée, dirty beans and rice, and gumbo. "What if we do something like this and share? I know it's going to be more than either of us can finish off, and it would give us several things to try. Not to mention leave room for dessert."

"I was thinking I might just get a bowl of French onion soup. It sounds amazing." No need to make him share his meal.

"You still could order that and then just take a few bites from mine. I think I'll get this no matter what because I want to try it all." He leaned back in his seat. "Besides, the person who pays gets to insist, right?"

"Oh, you don't have to—"

"It was my idea. And this is probably a bit more than you would have gone for otherwise, right?"

The waitress came to take their orders before she could reply. She ordered the soup, telling herself she wouldn't try any of his meal, no matter what. The soup would fill her up, and she'd somehow convince the waitress to let her pay for it too.

"So, you're from north of here, huh?" He twirled a straw through his fingers.

"Trying to find out personal information?" Katie made a show of smoothing her napkin in her lap. No need to meet his eyes.

"Just curious. It's always interesting to see where other vacationers come from." He tapped the table. "I know you're a librarian. That you're Bree's maid of honor. That you don't like some crowds but don't seem to mind others. That you've never had real Cajun food. And that you're from north of here."

"Seems like you know a lot about me after only a day and a half." She couldn't help smiling a little.

"You're also not allergic to fire ants. And you love history."

"What about you?" Time to change the direction of this conversation before she was tempted to share anything deeper. "All I know is that you're Ryan's cousin, your uncle paid for this trip, and you are a physical therapist and lifeguard."

"Actually, I'm not."

Her head jerked up and she saw his teasing smile. She frowned. "You're not what?"

"Not a physical therapist. And not a lifeguard for the past couple of years, although it would be easy to renew my certification." He straightened the saltshaker. "I'm an assistant football coach and health teacher. And I do some PRN work for an assisted living facility."

She shook her head. "PRN?"

"It basically means 'as needed.' I fill in and work with some of the residents when the rehab facility is short on staff."

"Then why did you tell me you were a physical therapist?"

"I didn't."

Trying to contain a groan, she slapped her hands on the table. "I know you hit my head, but you didn't hit it that hard. When I questioned you in the pool yesterday, that's what you said you were."

"No." He covered her hands before she could bang them again. "I said I had a degree in physical therapy. It comes in handy on the football field, trust me."

She slipped her fingers back out from beneath his before she gave in to the temptation to leave them there permanently. Not an option. This relationship had nowhere to go.

"These dishes are hot, so be careful." The waitress appeared, keeping their conversation from deepening for the moment. Amazing smells wafted from each dish, reminding Katie just how long it had been since they ate anything substantial. "Here's the extra plate you asked for. And some warm bread to top it off. Let me know if you need anything else."

Katie picked up her spoon and got ready to dip into the layer of melty cheese on top of her bowl, but Camden's hand stilled her.

"Pray with me first?"

She froze, gave a quick nod. She normally did offer a blessing before a meal but wasn't sure he was a believer too. Mentally she made a check next to his name on a list she hadn't even realized she'd started keeping.

"Thank you, God, for this amazing food. Thank you for the new friends Ryan and I made on this trip. Please bless the girls as they travel on tomorrow. And thank you for this short amount of time to get to know them. If it's your will, please let our paths cross in the future so we can get to know each other even more. Amen."

She swallowed a lump. He wanted to get to know her more too? But she couldn't dwell on that thought. This was a vacation thing. Only a few days and then done. Even if they exchanged phone numbers, they weren't likely to stay in touch.

"How's your soup?" Camden held out the basket of crusty bread to her.

Quickly, she took a bite and regretted her hastiness as the heat from the broth scalded her tongue. "Mm."

He pressed a glass of water in her hands. "So much for you tasting anything now, huh? Pretty sure you just burned off all your taste buds."

Another smile crept unbidden over her mouth. He made her smile more than any guy she'd met in the last few years. How was that fair?

After blowing on it for a few seconds, she tried another spoonful, more slowly this time. The tanginess of the onions and the saltiness of the broth melded perfectly with the tartness of the Swiss cheese and the crunchiness of the bread. She closed her eyes and enjoyed a deep breath as she finished the bite.

"That good, eh?" He held out his fork. "Want to try some of this? I haven't eaten from this side."

"What is it?" She passed him her own utensil. "I might try some beans and rice."

"It's good. The andouille is just right." He passed her fork back laden and steaming.

"Andouille?"

"It's a smoked sausage."

He was right. It was good.

They were quiet for several minutes, each lost in thoughts and delightful food, with him passing her bites from his platter every so often. Half a loaf of bread later, most of the food was gone and her tummy was much happier. She took a sip of water and scraped one more bite of cheese off her bowl.

"You haven't tried the étouffée." He held out a spoonful.

"What all's in it?" She raised an eyebrow. "It's not crawfish, is it?"

"No. I asked for the shrimp."

She wrinkled her nose. "I'm not terribly fond of those either."

"Same reason as before?"

She lifted one shoulder in a half shrug.

"Close your eyes."

———

Would she trust him? Camden held his breath as the emotions flickered across Katie's face. The ones he could read were doubt, fear, insecurity, maybe a little curiosity ... and trust? Finally, those lashes lowered, and she sat in front of him, waiting for whatever his plan was. His breath released and he barely kept himself from bouncing in his chair.

"Now open your mouth."

She hesitated and then inched her lips apart.

He slid the spoon of rice and shrimp into her mouth, trying not to be jealous of her silverware touching those lips. Her eyes fluttered open as he pulled his hand back, no more than a grain or two of rice left on the utensil.

"Good?" He raised an eyebrow, daring her to say, "No."

She chewed meticulously, but a small grin played around the corners of her mouth that intrigued him more with each moment. Curls bounced as she nodded. She ducked her head, but he could still see the full smile gracing her lovely face.

"They have bread pudding, I noticed on the menu." He leaned back. Maybe if he pretended he hadn't won that small battle, the bit of progress they'd made wouldn't be hampered.

"I'm not sure I could eat another bite right now. It was all so good, but I'm stuffed." She rubbed her flat belly and placed her napkin on the table.

"What if we get it to go? It's a gorgeous night, with a full moon in the sky. We could walk back to the hotel and sit by the pool for a while." He rested his forearms on the table, wondering if he was pressing his luck.

"Okay. Bread pudding does sound good."

His heart skipped a few beats in joy. Not only had she agreed to come tonight, but she'd also shown trust in letting him feed her that bite and she was okay with spending more time with him. This situation was crazy. Normally he wouldn't even look at a girl twice when he wasn't home, but this one had literally fallen in his arms. Was God trying to tell him something? The more time they spent together, the more Camden wanted to find out.

With a Styrofoam container emitting the heady aroma of cinnamon and sugar, two spoons, and to-go cups of coffee, they ambled the few blocks to their motel. He wasn't brave enough to reach out for her hand, but if his arm just happened to brush against hers a few times as they dodged other pedestrians, she wouldn't complain too much, right?

The night air was still humid, but not as thick as earlier in the day. The moon and security lights cast a blue glow over the pool area, but it was still unlocked, so they claimed two lounge chairs and leaned back to see the few stars visible through the city's light pollution.

"I think this has been my favorite vacation ever." He broke the silence, grinning over at her.

"Really?" She glanced away from the sky and over at him. "Why?"

"You."

She visibly stiffened. "Camden."

It was the first time she'd said his name, but he liked the sound of it on her tongue despite the hesitancy and caution her voice carried with it.

Before she could argue against anything, he held up the

dessert. "Ready for this now that we've walked off some of our dinner?"

She opened her mouth as if she were going to say something, then closed it again and accepted the spoon he offered. "Thanks."

"This is so good." The words came out jumbled around his mouthful of pudding. "Oh, man."

She laughed out loud, even leaning over, an arm against her stomach.

"You disagree?" He held his spoon out like a sword.

"No." She held her hands up. "It was just so funny to hear you say that. Just like my nephew would say something. And then his mama would chide him for talking with his mouth full."

"I didn't know you had a nephew."

She dug out another bite and chewed for a moment before answering. "My sister's son. He's three."

"I bet you're a fun aunt."

"What makes you say that?" She licked her spoon. "I haven't exactly been a bundle of laughs the last twenty-four hours."

"I don't know." He reached over and wiped a spot of caramel off the corner of her mouth. "I've seen your passion for history, your love of adventure, your ability to go along with a fun idea, and how absolutely you love your friends, no matter what."

She caught his hand as he rested it against her cheek. It felt so right, he mentally willed her to keep it there forever. She shook her head.

"You saw a lot more than was maybe even there." Her voice was barely a whisper.

"I don't think so." He leaned a tad closer. "You really wanted to go see a museum or a plantation or linger at the monuments and statues today ... because you know the history and it brings those things to life for you. But you also accepted that your friends weren't interested, so you swallowed your disappointment and went along with what they wanted to do instead.

"On the ferry this afternoon, I could tell you were thinking of all the stories about that river you'd ever read, reliving each and every scene you could think of. And even though Skye's been driving you crazy, you'd do anything for her."

The tiny gasp she released tickled the inside of his wrist. "What are we doing, Camden? This is like a fairy tale. Like living make-believe for a few days, but then we leave tomorrow and what? What's supposed to happen after that?"

"I don't know." He scooted slightly, so he was on the very edge of his chair. "But don't you think it's worth finding out?"

Her lips parted, and he could see the arguments running through her head. She didn't want to admit she might be interested. But she was weakening.

He moved in even more, at the verge of tipping his chair over, waiting to see if she'd be open to the idea of him closing the gap all the way. Her hand remained on top of his. She visibly swallowed and wet her lips. Everything stilled around them, and the only thing he could hear was her quickened breathing. Just another inch, and he could taste those lips that had been tempting him since dinner.

"I knew it!"

Skye's shriek of glee from across the courtyard had Katie jerking back and turning away from him again. His hand instantly missed the warmth of her touch. His breath released in a huge sigh. What awful timing.

"Thanks so much for dinner tonight." Katie handed him her spoon. "It was really good."

Before he could stop her, she dashed past her giggling

friend and up the stairs. Ryan raised an eyebrow, but Camden didn't want to face his cousin. Under normal circumstances it was Ryan making a move on a girl he'd just met. But there'd been something there, more than just a chance meeting on a road trip stop.

If only they'd had a few more moments! Would a kiss have convinced her to exchange phone numbers and see what they could work out further down the road? Camden dashed a hand through his hair and chucked the rest of the dessert in the trash can. He had no appetite for it now.

"I can give you her number, if you're interested." Skye held up her phone.

Tempting as that idea was, he resisted. "No. She didn't want me to have it. Until she does, it wouldn't be right."

"Sorry we obviously came back too early." Skye frowned. "I really was rooting for you."

"Don't worry about it. Like Katie said earlier, we were living in a fairy tale." Camden shook his head.

"Well, goodnight boys." Skye waved and then headed towards the girls' room.

"Relax, Cam." Ryan clapped him on the shoulder as they made their way up the stairs. "Skye and I have been talking, and I think I have a plan you're going to love. At least, you'll love it if we really did interrupt what it looked like we were interrupting."

"Ryan ..."

"No, seriously. Hear me out." Ryan unlocked their door and flopped down on the bed. "This is the best idea I've ever had."

# 6

Katie pushed her sunglasses higher on her nose. The sunshine played peek-a-boo behind the clouds, wreaking havoc with her tired eyes. She gripped the steering wheel tighter and focused on the interstate ahead.

The girls had risen early to hit the road. Even though Gulf Shores was only about three hours from New Orleans, they wanted as much time as possible to spend on the beach. Getting up before the sun wouldn't normally bother Katie, but she hadn't been able to fall asleep until almost three, her memory conjuring up a certain boy leaning in for a kiss every time she closed her eyes.

"Are you sure you're okay? I can drive if you want to nap." Bree looked at her from the passenger seat.

"I'm fine." Katie's voice came out more snappish than she meant.

There'd been no sign of the boys as she, Bree, and Skye loaded their car and pulled out. One more good thing about getting such an early start. Better to leave things as they were

57

and not be further tempted to pursue something that would never work.

"I know you didn't sleep much." Bree's hand tentatively touched Katie's arm. "Want to talk about it?"

"No."

"I could text Ryan and get his number for you." Skye leaned forward from the backseat. "I know he'd be willing to pass it on."

"Leave it alone." Katie squeezed the words through clenched teeth, refusing to look in the rearview mirror for fear she might let out some of the mean things running through her head. "It was just a fun day with a cute guy who I'll never see again. Move on."

"How do you know you'll never see him again?" Skye tapped her fingers on Katie's seat.

Katie's gaze left the road to glance at her friend's reflection. Skye raised her eyebrows in a look that was supposed to be innocent but came across far more self-satisfied and gleeful. Movement in the mirror caught her eye—a familiar car zipped around the semi-truck behind them and pulled ahead, whipping into the spot just behind their convertible.

"What did you do?" Katie forced her eyes back on the road ahead, just in time to see the dead possum in the middle of the lane. "Ah!"

*Clunk.*

The bump made her grimace. She hated hitting animals even if they were already deceased. If she hadn't been distracted by her meddling friend and the co-conspirator driving behind them, she'd have easily avoided the feel of roadkill under the tires.

"What?" Bree grabbed the dashboard. "What did we just hit?"

"A possum." Katie slapped her hand against the steering wheel. "But that's not the biggest pest in this area."

"Katie? What are you talking about?" Bree glanced over her shoulder at Skye.

"Skye has evidently been making plans behind our backs." Katie ground her teeth until she was sure they'd be a full millimeter shorter.

"Skye?" Bree's voice held a sense of foreboding. And well it should. So much for this being a girls' trip. Skye just couldn't keep her mouth shut. Couldn't leave well enough alone. For the first time, Katie was glad this was the last time they'd ever do this. She never wanted to see Skye again after Bree's wedding.

Half an hour later, a sign for a rest area gave her a reason to pull off for a few minutes. Although it might also afford her the opportunity to shake Skye until her teeth rattled. It was a risk she'd have to take. She pulled into a parking lot, cut the engine, and headed up the sidewalk toward the restrooms before anyone could catch her. Sooner or later, she'd have to face them all, but she needed a few moments to cool off first.

Several minutes later, the door banged open followed by Bree's voice. "Katie?"

Even though she knew it wouldn't hide her for long, Katie pulled her feet back from the edge of the stall.

"Katie, we know you're in here. Come out and talk to me." Bree's shoes stopped right in front of her, and the handle rattled.

"Give me a few more minutes, please." Katie's voice choked as she finished her plea. But she couldn't help it. Nothing about this trip had gone as she expected. Part of her wanted to find a plane and fly home now instead of sticking it out the rest of the week. At least back home, she'd be away from her well-meaning 'friends,' who kept pushing her out of her comfort zone.

"I'll be right outside."

"Just you?"

"Just me." Bree tapped the metal frame a couple times as if she wished she were patting Katie on the shoulder.

Katie swallowed, closed her eyes, and inhaled several deep gulps of air. How could she go out there, knowing Camden would be there too? After she'd left him the way she did last night. After that almost-kiss.

And how could she ever trust Skye again? From the very first evening, Skye had turned this into a girls' *and guys'* trip. So much for this being a bachelorette week for Bree. Skye had practically ignored the bride and spent all her time with Ryan.

Katie splashed some water on her face and took another deep breath. *I will not kill Skye. I will not kill Skye. I will not kill Skye.* Maybe if she repeated it enough times in her head ... she'd at least limit herself to one punch instead of multiple?

She shook her head. That wasn't much better. She forced her clenched fingers to relax. The muggy Mississippi air accosted her as she stepped back outside and joined Bree sitting on a bench by the building. Skye leaned against their car, talking to Ryan. Camden was nowhere to be seen.

"She ruined our trip." Katie's voice came out much whinier than she intended.

"It's not ruined. She just changed it a bit." Bree leaned against Katie.

"She didn't even warn us. Just invited the boys along whether we wanted them or not." Katie shook her head. "What is Nathan going to say when he hears that two guys spent the whole week with us after we told him he couldn't come? Didn't you mention earlier that the thought of two guys accompanying us yesterday upset him?"

"I assured him they're both interested in my friends. And even though he says he wishes he were here, too, I don't know how he'd do as a tourist with no concrete plan. He's not the greatest at going with the flow." Bree shrugged. "But Nathan knows I love him and only him."

Skye walked up, a slight look of sheepishness across her face. "Are you furious with me?"

"It's taking every ounce of self-control I have to not bust your perfect nose in." Katie tucked her hands under her thighs to prove her point.

"Look, Katie Belle." Skye glanced over her shoulder and then back. "I didn't actually mean to let him know the rest of our plans. They just sort of slipped out. And when he mentioned he didn't have anything planned for the rest of the week, and we saw the attraction growing between you and Camden, we thought it might be a good idea to give you guys more time together. I was just trying to help, honest."

"I didn't come on this trip to meet a guy. I came on this trip to spend time with my girlfriends. It's not like we'll get to do this anymore once Bree's married and I start working. This was our last chance. And now we can't even do that because you keep dragging them into it." Katie stood and poked Skye in the shoulder. "And I don't want the attraction to grow between Camden and me. I don't need a boyfriend, so quit pushing."

Skye's eyes widened as she looked over Katie's shoulder. Before Katie even turned, she knew Camden stood behind her, his lips pressed tightly and his arms crossed.

---

"For the record, this wasn't my idea." He tucked his disappointment away for later, when he would be alone. For now, he just needed to survive the rest of the week with what remained of his heart intact.

Skye and Bree backed away, leaving Katie alone in front of him. She looked slightly guilty about the harsh words she'd half-shouted at her friend, but he didn't expect her to take them back either. She pulled her sunglasses from where they sat tucked in the curls on top of her head and covered her eyes. Now he couldn't read them at all.

"Ryan kidnapped you, did he?" Her voice dripped sarcasm.

"I told you. I'm along for the ride. Uncle John is paying for this trip, and Ryan had already squared it with him to go to Gulf Shores today before he even mentioned his plans to me." Camden forced his arms to uncross and tucked his hands in his pockets.

"And this is keeping him out of trouble?" Katie waved her hand around. "Because you don't seem to have much influence when it comes to your cousin. I'm beginning to wonder why your uncle trusted you for this job."

"I've wondered the whole time, but evidently, I'm considered trustworthy. At least to some people." Camden kicked a piece of mulch back into one of the flower beds. "Look, I'll try to keep him from following you to wherever your last stop is. He hasn't passed that information on. And I'll stay out of your way while you're here. Sorry to have ruined your trip."

He breezed past, careful not to bump into her on the narrow path. After all, she didn't want to be attracted to him, so there was no point in getting any closer than absolutely necessary. As he approached, Ryan, Bree, and Skye straightened from where they'd been huddled together between the two cars.

"Ryan, let's just go back to New Orleans. We're not that far away now. Or we could even go somewhere else." Camden pulled up a map on his phone.

"What?" Ryan twirled the car keys around his finger. "No way."

"Ryan, seriously. We can't just barge into their plans. Maybe you and Skye can meet up when they're finished with their trip." Camden crossed his arms again. Why did he have the be the reasonable and responsible one?

"You're giving up?" Ryan snapped. "Just like that?"

"Giving up?" Camden threw his hands up in the air. "Are you kidding? You're forcing something that isn't there. Leave well enough alone, and let's get out of their way."

"No." Ryan planted his feet. "If you don't want to come, you can find a ride home. It's only, what? Eight hours or so from here?"

"More like six." Camden rolled his eyes at Ryan's lack of a sense of direction.

"So even less. My offer stands. You can come with me, or you can find a way to get home." Ryan's jaw was set firm, and Camden knew he wouldn't give in. Uncle John had trusted him to keep Ryan from too much trouble. He'd be letting him down if he went home now.

"You might as well come." Katie's voice made Camden turn his head. "Looks like he's as stubborn as she is."

"See? She wants you to come too." Skye smiled as if every problem had been solved.

"That's not what she said." Bree's whisper was loud enough to be heard by them all. "Seriously, Skye. Stop already!"

"Look, it's not like they're going to be staying in Aunt Heather's condo with us." Skye propped a hand on her hip. "They've got their own hotel somewhere down the road. You can't tell someone they can't go to a public beach."

"Well, she's not wrong about that." Ryan twirled his keys once more. "Let's go soak up some sun!"

"Bree's turn to drive." Skye climbed in the passenger seat.

Katie had already crawled into the back. Skye pressed a button and their roof retracted as Camden slid back into Ryan's vehicle.

"I still say this isn't a good idea." Camden lowered the sunshade on his side to block the glare.

"That girl just needs to relax." Ryan revved their engine and then pulled out right behind the girls. "I bet the beach is going to loosen her up enough for you to get that kiss we interrupted last night."

"I'm not even going to try again." Camden closed his eyes, hoping if he pretended to sleep, his cousin would leave him alone for the last hour of their drive. "She's not interested."

"She's just too stubborn to admit it. Keep working on her. Skye says Katie is too serious and needs to have more fun."

"You and Skye seem to be having enough fun for all of us." Camden crossed one foot over the other, leaning his chair back a few more inches.

"A person can never have too much fun."

"Bet."

"All right." Ryan tapped the steering wheel in rhythm with the beat of the music. "I'll take that bet. You try having as much fun as Skye and I have been and see if it's too much or not. And I'll keep having as much fun and *prove* it's not too much."

"That's not even something you can measure. You can't bet on something like that." Camden opened one eye.

"I'll help you finish your deck when you get home if you win."

"Ryan, are you listening to me? You can't bet on something that can't be proven." Camden shook his head. "But you're more than welcome to help me finish my deck, regardless. It's the least you can do after dragging me through all this."

"Dragging you on vacation. Oh, boo hoo." Ryan's voice

mocked. "Poor cousin Camden not having to pay to go enjoy New Orleans and the Gulf Coast. Not to mention time with pretty ladies."

"Pretty ladies with no desire to spend time with me." Camden swallowed down another ounce of regret at Katie's harsh words earlier. Was she really not interested, or simply trying to keep her heart from getting broken? He understood that desire more than anyone.

"I bet she proves different when we actually get there."

"You're just full of bets today, aren't you?" Camden stared out his window, catching a glimpse every now and then of the sparkling blue gulf in the distance. "And whose money are you betting?"

"Come on, Cam. Can't you just go along with this for now? I thought I was helping you. You've been so gloomy the last few years, and Katie seemed to bring out the you that was fun to hang out with."

"Yeah, well, Katie doesn't need to know that, okay?" Camden worked his jaw back and forth. "She told Bree she's not interested. So, you and Skye can have fun, but I'll stay out of Katie's way."

"Suit yourself." Ryan shrugged. "But I think you're wrong."

"And who made you all-knowing in the love department?"

"No one. But she definitely didn't look uninterested last night." Ryan snickered and followed Bree as she veered off to the south in Mobile.

"I've been through it with a girl who didn't look uninterested before. Remember?" Camden clenched and unclenched his fingers. "It didn't turn out so well."

"Jen—"

"Don't say her name." Camden pushed his seat back all the way. "I don't want to talk about it anymore." He closed his eyes and turned his head away.

Ryan was quiet, which was what Camden had been hoping for, but now he was stuck in his own head. And this conversation had left nothing but regrets and ghosts swirling through his thoughts. It was just as well Katie didn't want to try and pursue anything. His heart couldn't handle much more.

# 7

"Oh, my!" Skye pointed the opposite direction from where they were supposed to be heading. "Pull over! Check this out!"

Bree whipped into a parking lot and leaned over. A large warehouse-style store stood in front of them, a humongous shark on the front.

"Isn't it the most?" Skye had opened her door and exited before Bree or Katie could reply.

The guys parked beside them and leaned down to study the structure through their windshield. Katie caught Camden's eyes, and they both exchanged a look of disbelief before he quickly averted his gaze. A shot of disappointment struck her heart. Besides Bree, Camden had understood her better than anyone else this trip. Maybe even better than Bree, considering how distracted her best friend was by all her wedding plans.

"Come on!" Skye waved at them from inside the shark's mouth. "We've got to take a picture."

"You know she won't give up until we actually do this, right?" Bree glanced over her shoulder.

"I know." Katie crawled out behind her, and they strolled over to their bubbly friend.

"Come on. Come on!" Skye tugged their arms and pulled them into the giant mouth with her. "Ryan can snap the photo for us."

Katie smiled at the camera, knowing Skye wouldn't be happy until she got the perfect shot. And, in forcing her smile, she found it coming more naturally after a few moments of the laugh-worthy situation. This was the kind of fun thing they'd done on their other trips. Though, Katie recalled, Skye had found funny photo ops in New Orleans. She'd simply chosen to take those photos with Ryan instead of the girls.

"Shall we park at Aunt Heather's and change into swim-suits?" Skye practically skipped back to the car, obviously not intending to step a foot into the souvenir shop fronted by the shark. "I'm ready for some beach time."

"Your hotel probably won't let you check in this early." Bree looked at the guys. "Why don't you park where we're staying, and you can change in one of the other rooms? We're only a block from the beach."

"Sure." Ryan waved them on. "I'll follow you."

Skye's aunt's condo looked more like an apartment from the outside, but the inside was airy, with tall curtains, various shades of light blue and cream, and bamboo floors. Everyone paused and caught their breaths at the balcony's view. The turquoise water beyond the white sand beach sent its steady, pounding rhythm through the air and into Katie's heart.

"Okay. Now I'm even more ready." Skye dashed up the stairs with her smallest suitcase and slammed a door. Katie could only guess she was changing into swimwear.

Katie walked up at a more leisurely pace, peeking into the room still open. A second bedroom followed the overall color scheme, but a large sunset ocean print hung on the wall over the bed. Maybe Katie wasn't so upset to be stopping here for a day, after all. She waited for Bree before closing the door and digging out her tankini and board shorts.

"Do you think Skye will want to leave tomorrow after this?" Katie double-knotted the halter straps behind her neck.

"She said something about her aunt needing the condo later in the week, so this is all the time we'd have anyway. Besides, I know you want to get to Jodie's house tomorrow afternoon and love on that nephew." Bree held out a bottle of sunscreen and turned so Katie could do her back. "We all agreed on this plan before we left."

"True." Katie rubbed the cream into Bree's fair skin and turned so her friend could return the favor. "Still. It does feel a bit heavenly here, doesn't it? Why haven't we taken advantage of this connection before?"

"No time. All the other trips, we had reasons for going where we did." Bree grabbed her flipflops and returned to the condo's living area.

At the bottom of the steps, Katie's foot slipped, and she pitched forward. Strong arms caught her around the waist and set her gently on the ground. She turned and came face to face with Camden's bare chest.

"You seem to be making a habit of catching me." How the words squeezed out around the lump in her throat, she had no idea.

"My pleasure." His voice was just above a whisper. He cleared his throat and moved around her. "I was just grabbing my towel."

Katie gathered her own towel and necessities into a large mesh bag with the other girls' things. Together, they walked the block and paused on the edge of the sand, taking in the view. Katie had never seen an ugly beach, but something about the Gulf Coast always moved her in a way no other had. The sand was white, and, for a long stretch, the clear aquamarine water was almost always warm and shallow.

"Ooh. Paddleboards!" Skye grabbed Ryan's arm and tugged him toward a rental booth.

"Are either of you interested in that?" Camden pointed at the other two.

Katie held up a hand. "No coordination. As I'm sure you've noticed."

"I just want to sit under that unoccupied umbrella over there and read for a while." Bree held up her e-reader.

"Perfect." Katie jumped at the excuse to not be adventurous like Skye.

Katie and Bree settled themselves on a big blanket Bree had found at the condo, their legs stretched out behind them. Kids ran by, shells in their hands. Couples meandered along the shoreline, hand in hand. Katie held a book in front of her, but her eyes kept straying elsewhere. To a long, lanky guy walking toward the pier, to be exact.

What was wrong with her? Hadn't she pushed him away over and over again? And now she was seeking him out?

"Why don't you go after him?" Bree nudged her with her foot.

"Who?" Katie turned a page, despite the fact she hadn't read a word.

"Go on. Go after him. You obviously want to."

"I'm supposed to be spending time with you this week." Katie rolled onto her side. "I mean, you won't even live close enough to visit very often after you marry Nathan. We've got to soak this up."

"Katie, I love you. You're the best friend I've ever had." Bree put both hands on either side of Katie's face and squeezed. "But I know you didn't mean it when you said you weren't interested in him. What's holding you back from seeing if he might be your Nathan?"

Katie shook off her friend's hands. "Bree, you're so happy in love that you think everyone else needs to be too. But I'm very content with my new job at the library. Maybe someday in the future, I'll find someone as amazing as you have. But allowing myself to fall in love with someone I'll only know a few days? That's not realistic."

"But if you guys thought it might develop into something, you could exchange numbers." Bree sat up and crossed her legs. "You don't even know where he lives, do you? What if he lives closer to you than you think?"

"What would be the odds of that?" Katie shook her head but couldn't resist another glimpse over her shoulder. "Things like that never happen to me."

"Maybe they don't happen because you won't let them." Bree nudged her arm. "Go on. At least go apologize for the fit you threw when you found out they were coming too. Otherwise, we're all going to be awkward the rest of the time here. And the beach has no room for awkwardness. At least not that kind. Now, awkward swimsuits ..." Bree motioned her head toward a scantily clad woman with an obvious wedgie.

Katie smiled and nodded. Should she take her friend's advice? Skye and Ryan laughed together out in the waves as he helped her stand upright on the board. Camden was no longer in sight. Had he gone out on the pier? She slid a bookmark in her novel and set it next to Bree.

"I'll be back."

"Take your time." Bree lifted her e-reader again, a smirk on her lips.

Two tan legs slid down beside Camden as he occupied a bench on the pier. He clamped down the leap his heart made. She'd come after him?

"I thought I'd have to go all the way to the end before I found you." Katie studied the water below them. "This is the longest pier I've ever seen."

"I think it's the biggest in the gulf." Small talk. She came after him for small talk? He could play that game, too. "Do you fish?"

"Only if someone else will bait my hook." She kicked her legs back and forth, her feet barely grazing the wooden boards below them. It hadn't been the answer he was expecting.

"Really?"

"I hate baiting a hook. The thought of sticking that sharp point through cricket or worm." She wrinkled her nose. "And you already know how I feel about what fish and other under-water creatures eat."

She was adorable. He looked back out at the water and the people enjoying it. Anything to keep from growing closer to her.

"I just didn't expect you to like fishing at all." He swatted at an insect buzzing his ears.

"Because I'm a librarian?"

"No. I don't know."

"We used to go over to my grandpa's farm and fish in his pond. He kept it stocked with catfish. One time, though, my sister caught a turtle instead. He was so mad."

"Your grandpa was mad?" He couldn't keep his eyes off her.

"No. The turtle." She grinned at him, then looked down. "Listen, I ... I'm no good at this, but I need to apologize."

He didn't say anything, afraid to break the spell. Would she apologize for saying she didn't want to see where this thing between them might go? For running away so fast last night? For what?

She took a deep breath and fixed her gaze somewhere in the direction of Orange Beach. "I don't handle change well. I guess you can tell. When Skye messed—" She shook her head. "When Skye decided to include two more in our plans, it wasn't what I had fixed in my head, and I freaked. Obviously. But you didn't deserve all the things I said earlier. I was really mad at Skye more than anyone."

No mention of remorse over last night or her words about not being interested, but it was a start. He stood. "Did you want to walk to the end of the pier?"

She looked that direction, craned her neck, and then shook her head. "Nope. I'm good. We're at the beach. We should be walking through the waves though, right?"

"Sounds good to me." He headed toward the sand.

What was the protocol for this situation? Who was he kidding? There wasn't any. No one else in the world got into messes like this. Insanely attracted to a girl he'd just met days before but unsure if she had even an inkling of interest. And knowing he shouldn't act on the attraction, regardless.

Minute by minute. That's how he'd take the rest of the day. No need to try and live beyond that anyway. This was supposed to be a vacation.

Warm sand oozed into his flipflops as they stepped onto the beach. She wandered toward the ocean's edge and walked in the wet sand, giggling as the water rolled up and covered her toes every few seconds. He pulled her close as a frisbee whizzed right where she'd been standing a second before.

"Two saves in one day. Thanks." She glanced up at him and he realized his arm was still wrapped around her. She smelled like sunscreen and something else he couldn't quite put a finger on. Nothing overpowering, but strong enough to linger after he released her. Maybe one of her hair products?

"Here's a starfish." He quickly focused on the first thing he could find that wasn't her.

She leaned down and reached out a tentative finger to the crusty-looking body. "Poor guy. Washed up on shore and all dried out."

"Do you collect seashells?" He handed her a small, pearly conch-style one.

"Bree does." She glanced in the direction of her friend. "Let's go see if she wants to join us. I can't imagine her wanting to read the whole day away."

"Sure." Maybe with another person around, there wouldn't be so much tension between them.

But Bree was snoozing when they reached her. Katie adjusted the umbrella so that her friend was mostly shaded and then shrugged at him. So much for that idea. Skye and Ryan were no longer playing nearby with a paddleboard, but he figured they hadn't gone far.

He and Katie continued their trek down the shoreline, gathering a few of the more perfect shells for Bree. They stopped farther down the beach and helped with a particularly tricky sandcastle project where the builder couldn't quite reach the top. Waving at Ryan and Skye, they made their way back toward Bree.

"Does Ryan work?" Katie sidestepped a jellyfish that had washed ashore. Her nose wrinkled once again.

"Not yet. He has one more year of college." Camden glanced up as a cloud covered the sunshine for a minute. The sky was looking more grey and white than blue now. Something to keep an eye on. "At least, that's the plan. Unless he changes his mind again."

"Perpetual student?"

"Not ready to grow up, I think."

"Sounds like Skye. She graduated with us last week but hasn't done anything about lining up work or a place to live outside her father's house." Katie kicked the foamy water as it rushed towards her. "I can't imagine not having a plan. A goal."

"Yeah. Things were always tight at my house growing up. There was never really a question of me moving back in once I finished school." A larger wave crashed into the shore and knocked her into his side. "You good?"

"Fine. Just wasn't expecting that." She scanned the waves that were choppier now. "It's getting a little rough out there."

"The sky too." He pointed at several lines of grey clouds that had inched closer over the last few minutes. "Maybe we should head back."

"Oh." Katie's eyes widened. "Yes. All right. I didn't realize how far we'd walked. Can you even see the others?"

"Not from here, but if we need to, we can meet them back at the condo, right?" He didn't like the fear in her voice.

"Yes." She rubbed one of the shells between her fingers.

"Hey." He wrapped an arm around her shoulders and pulled her to his side. "It's okay. Just some rain."

She nodded but leaned into him more as another wave slapped against her legs.

"Let's walk a little farther up so the water doesn't keep beating you." He steered her through the clearing beach. The umbrella edges flapped, sea oats waved in the gusty wind, and mamas hurried their children toward the parking lots and hotels.

Katie caught his attention and pointed to their friends heading toward the condo, half a mile down the beach. He turned her that direction too. No point walking all the way down there when they could cut the corner and shorten the distance.

Big, fat raindrops hit his shoulders and head all at once. Katie shrieked and laughed as they picked up the pace. Their flipflops slapped the bottoms of their feet as they dashed down the rapidly dampening streets. The sky's moisture escalated quickly to a steady drencher. A big clap of thunder sounded overhead as they reached the building's overhang.

"Whew!" Katie ran a hand through her curls, knocking water out and moving them from her eyes. "So much for spending all day on the beach."

"There you are!" Bree opened the door and pulled them both inside. "We were hoping you'd just come here instead of trying to find us in all that chaos."

"We saw you heading this way as we made our way back." Camden accepted his towel from Ryan.

"Ryan suggested running out to get burgers and then hanging out here this afternoon." Skye came down the stairs, her hair in a towel. "If I remember correctly, Aunt Heather has games stashed around here somewhere. But the fridge is empty."

An afternoon stuck spending more time with Katie? His heart screamed *yes*, but his mind yelled *no*. He ignored them both. What other choice did he have? They couldn't check in to their hotel until three. And hanging out with Katie sounded so much better than sitting in the rain, even if the latter might be the safer alternative.

# 8

"Does your aunt play poker or something? There's like fifteen different decks of cards in here." Katie looked over to where Ryan dug through the closet under the stairs.

"No. We like to play Nerts when our family's all down here." Skye walked over and gathered several different packs. "Who's in?"

"Nerts?" Camden gathered lunch trash from the living room and tossed it in the garbage.

"Sort of like multiplayer solitaire on steroids." Katie knelt in front of the coffee table. "It can be intense."

"I'm all for intense." Ryan shuffled a blue-backed set.

"Are they all different so we can keep score?" Bree sat beside Katie.

"Yes. I think there's some paper around here somewhere." Skye was back at the closet, digging through old boxes of board games and old beach toys.

Another clap of thunder rumbled outside, reminding Katie why they were cooped up in here. She cast a glance over her shoulder toward the window, but then returned to her deck. It

77

was decorated with a rooster on the back. She mixed the cards loosely in her hands, shuffling them until they were ready to start.

"So, explain the rules exactly?" Camden took Katie's other side, and she willed her heartbeat to stay normal. They'd gotten along just fine that morning, even with him putting his arm around her several times. There was no reason for his close proximity to have this effect on her now. They were just enjoying a temporary friendship today. That was all.

"Just like in Solitaire, you play sequential cards on top of others. But in this one, you'll have thirteen cards." She pulled thirteen cards from his deck, carefully avoiding any skin contact. "This is the pile you're trying to get rid of before anyone else gets rid of theirs."

"You can play on your four cards in front of you, or if someone draws an ace, they throw it in the middle, and anyone can play on it. You want as many cards in the middle as possible because that's where your score is going to come from. First one to empty their pile of thirteen yells Nerts, and all playing stops." Bree pointed out the various spots as she explained. "It's fairly easy to catch on, but it moves fast. Especially with us. We used to play in the dorm all the time."

"This and Spoons." Skye joined them with an old yellow tablet and pencil. "Thanks for getting my deck ready, Bree. I found some candy too." She placed a bowl of multi-colored chocolates on the end of the table that was likely to be safe from their play.

"I think I understand, but can we have a practice round first?" Camden flipped the edge of the cards in his hand as he studied the table.

"You chicken, Camden?" Katie raised an eyebrow.

"Of you?" One corner of his mouth turned up. "You have no idea."

"One practice round." Skye declared. "Starting ... now!"

Katie immediately began flipping her cards and playing any and all she could, throwing two different aces in the middle, right off the bat. That would help things. She didn't look at him outright but could sense the motion going on beside her. It was speeding up. Camden was smart. He'd catch on quickly, so she couldn't let him distract her.

Less than five minutes later, Bree yelled, "Nerts!"

A groan tore from Katie as she counted five left in her pile. That would hurt her score. She quickly jumped in to help sort the ones in the middle and then taught Camden how to score as she did her own. She grabbed a handful of candy between the rounds and sorted it by color. She always ate the blues first because that seemed the least natural hue.

"Did you just organize your chocolate?" Camden glanced over.

"Maybe." She popped another piece in her mouth.

"She can't even let go of controlling how she eats snacks." Skye giggled as she shuffled her cards. "Would you be able to eat them straight out of the package, or would you have to pour them out so you could eat them by color order?"

Katie shrugged. No point egging Skye on. She needed no extra encouragement.

"She does the same thing with the fruity ones. And the peanut butter ones too." Bree smiled at her. "But the peanut butter are her favorites."

"Fewer colors." Katie counted out her cards for the next round.

"I like the peanut butter ones too." Camden whispered directly in her ear. "But I eat the brown ones first."

She cut her eyes over his way. He sorted candy by color too? According to Skye's continual teasing, it was a control-freak thing to do, and normal people simply ate whatever color they drew from the package.

He winked.

Focus. The middle of a Nerts tournament was no place to lose one's head. And she didn't even want to consider how bad it would be to lose her heart. No.

She forced her attention back to the game. Time to kick things into higher gear with her rooster cards. She popped a red candy this time.

Three rounds later, Camden and Ryan were on their knees, leaning over and putting their full bodies into the game, just like the girls. Taunts and triumphs were called out as people beat each other to play a card a second before someone else could.

"Quit speaking voodoo over my cards.'" Skye wagged a finger at Bree, making her voice sound like the palm reader from New Orleans.

Groans and laughter filled the room.

Katie flipped her last card and saw the place it could go. She and Camden simultaneously reached for the same spot. She moved her shoulder to block him, and he raised up to his full height to reach around her.

"No." She batted at his hand to keep him away.

"But I haven't won yet. It's my turn." He poked her in the side, hitting a ticklish spot.

She shrieked and shifted to block him with her hips. Instead, her momentum toppled them both into the table, knocking cards in every direction.

Everyone's protests sounded above their laughter, and then Skye yelled, "Nerts!"

"Oh!" Katie groaned from where she'd slid onto the floor.

Camden's laughing eyes were right in front of her. They

caught hers and intensified. She swallowed and pressed her lips together.

"You two coming back up or should we go in the other room and give you some privacy?" Ryan's voice pulled her out of the moment.

Katie and Camden sat up at the same time and bumped heads. "Ow!"

Trying it again, Katie still couldn't move with him pressed against her. He caught her shoulders in his hands to still her, then shimmied himself out of the narrow space between the table and the couch. Once upright, he leaned down and helped her stand.

"Okay?" He picked up several cards that had scattered onto the rug.

"Fine." She straightened her shirt. "I just wish you'd quit bonking me in the head."

"Here are your cards." Bree's eyes held a hint of mischief and amusement as she held out the stack.

"Thanks." Katie slid back down to her knees. "I'm glad we weren't playing Spoons. Someone could have gotten seriously hurt the way we play."

Skye giggled. "Remember that one night when I ended up with fourteen bruises up and down my legs?"

"Good grief. What on earth did you do?" Camden tapped his deck against the table and wrote down his score.

"We put the spoons on the other side of the room from where we were playing." Bree dealt her next round. "That way we had to race to get them instead of just grabbing them from the middle. Except that night, we ended up tackling more than racing."

"It was definitely a good thing it was after curfew. Several of the girls in that building would've been furious if we'd used the lobby like that during the daytime. It would've interrupted their cuddle time with their boyfriends." Katie rolled her eyes.

"Where did you go to school?" Ryan asked.

"Freed-Hardeman University." Bree riffled through her cards as she waited for the others to be ready. "Tiny little Christian university in east Tennessee."

"One of our cousins went there." Camden nodded. "She loved it."

"We loved it too." Bree smiled. "I definitely made the best friends ever while I was there."

"Yeah. And Bree met the love of her life too." Skye shook her head. "She definitely got the best deal of all of us."

"But if you'd found the love of your life, you wouldn't have invited us to hang out with you." Camden smirked a little. "Right?"

"True. Maybe it's just as well none of my college boyfriends worked out." Skye tossed her hair over her shoulder. "Ready to start?"

The lights flickered as another rumble sounded outside. They'd been so wrapped up in their game they hadn't noticed the storm raging beyond the windows. The electricity went out, and all fell silent. Despite it being the middle of the afternoon, the condo was too dim to play cards. Lightning lit everything for a mere second, and Skye rose.

"Time to find candles or flashlights or something."

"Were there any in the game closet?" Katie hopped up to help.

"Anyone got the weather on their phone?" Bree tapped hers but evidently didn't have any bars.

"Yeah. Looks like it's almost passed." Camden held his out to her, the screen lighting up their faces.

Katie scanned the semi-dark room. "First one to find the candles wins."

"Wins what?" Camden's voice teased, but his face held interest deeper than a simple trophy.

"Gets to cook dinner for all of us, of course." Katie tried to make her words light and playful to hide the emotions roiling stronger than the storm outside.

"Hmm." Camden nodded and pointed down the hall. "I bet they're this way."

"Probably." Katie followed him to the kitchen.

---

Footsteps sounded upstairs where the others had gone to search for matches and candles, but Camden ignored them. Only one person in this condo held his attention. She dug through a drawer in the island, muttering about too many old pencils and twist ties. Her curls were wild this afternoon from where they'd gotten caught in the rain earlier. The tank top and shorts she'd changed into were just as appealing as her modest swimsuit had been.

"Aren't you going to look? Or did you think I was serious about cooking?" She looked up with a grin that made his breath come short. "What?"

"Oh. Sure." He opened the drawer next to him and held up the box of matches right in the front. "Ta da."

Her laugh rang out louder than the fading thunder and rain. "Nice."

She picked up a pillar candle from above the sink and brought it to him. He struck a match against the box and held it to the wick. The flame flared and then held, wavering only slightly in their mingled breath.

The glow caught in her eyes, but he couldn't read their depths. What was she thinking? Did she feel the ... something ... pulling them together again and again?

"We found some candles." Skye skipped into the kitchen and stopped abruptly. "Sorry. I keep interrupting, don't I?"

"Nope." Katie set their glowing candle on the counter. "We were just lighting the one we found. Camden has the matches."

Katie escaped quickly down the hallway. It took every ounce of Camden's willpower to refrain from following. But he exercised self-control. Hadn't he told himself only this morning that getting any deeper with her was a bad idea? And yet she was irresistible, despite the risk to his heart.

"She's skittish." Skye took her now-lighted candle and stepped back. "Not an easy one to catch."

"I don't know what you're talking about." Camden closed the box of matches and returned it to the drawer. He carried the first candle into the living room and set it on the mantle just as the power flicked back on again. Nothing like timing.

"The rain's tapering off." Katie stared out the door to the patio. "We could probably get out for dinner with no problems."

"Afraid of my cooking?" Camden stood as close to her as he dared.

"No. I just figured you wouldn't want to." Katie didn't even glance at him.

"I'll have you know I make a mean fajita. Assuming Aunt Heather has the right pan, we could do something easy like that and eat like kings."

"Fajitas?" Ryan bounded down the stairs. "Yes!"

"I'll run to the store." Camden grabbed the keys by the door and headed out into the light drizzle. Maybe half an hour away from the temptation would clear both their heads.

The store wasn't set up like the one back home, but he knew how to find things. Into the cart went chicken, peppers and onions, tortillas, and chips and salsa. On a whim, he added marshmallows, chocolate, and graham crackers. The fireplace was gas, and he had a hunch that s'mores would taste good after a rainy afternoon.

A love song played on the sound system and intruded into his stewing. It was one Jennifer had loved, but for the first time in two years, his chest didn't hurt to hear it.

He paid for the groceries and loaded everything into Ryan's car. Just like Katie, this vacation hadn't turned out as he'd expected. But he honestly couldn't complain about most of it. If only ...

*If only* never got anyone anywhere. He shook the thought from his head and focused on what he needed to do to fix dinner. He'd get through tonight and then convince Ryan the girls needed to go on without them. If Katie had no desire to see what might come of the possibilities between them, nothing he could do would change the outcome.

Aunt Heather turned out to have just the right pans and seasonings. He chopped onions and peppers with a zeal dangerous to the tips of his fingers. But somehow, he came out with all digits intact. Before long he had the meat and veggies sizzling in the hot skillet, the aroma filling the kitchen. Nothing soothed his soul like cooking.

"What can I do to help?" Bree leaned on the other side of the island.

"I think I've got it under control." He threw a towel over his shoulder.

"I wasn't talking about dinner." Bree's voice was lowered, just loud enough for him to make out above the sounds of the sautéing meat.

Should he ignore her? Pretend like he hadn't heard?

"Sorry." Bree came up beside him. "I know I shouldn't meddle, but she's my best friend. And for all I can tell, there's some real potential between you two. Is she scaring you off?"

"She's not encouraging anything. And I won't push it. She's right. This is just a vacation ... crush, if you will. We don't need to let it get too deep." He flipped some of the chicken and moved the peppers around.

"If you change your mind, let me know." She patted his arm. "I'll set the table."

The atmosphere was strained at the dinner table in spite of the amazing food. Camden made sure not to sit next to Katie. The more distance between them, the better. Ryan and Skye were quieter than normal too.

"These are amazing, Camden." Bree rolled a tortilla around another helping of chicken and veggies. "I bet we could all take one more walk on the beach this evening."

"Won't the tide be coming in?" Katie licked some salsa off her fingers, distracting Camden for a moment.

"The tides go out at night. Back in tomorrow morning." Skye munched a chip. "If we go walk when the tide's going out, sometimes you can find really neat shells, Bree. I'm up for it."

"Sure." Katie nodded. "I could use a walk before we're stuck in a car for so long tomorrow."

"Where are you going this time?" Ryan's voice held no humor like normal. Instead, it sounded rather dull. What was going on?

"I've been ordered not to tell you." Skye pushed her plate back. "After all, it upsets Katie when things change suddenly, and we can't have that."

Katie's lips pressed together, and she set the last few bites of her fajita on her plate.

"Skye." Bree's voice chided.

"What?" Skye pushed her chair back. "You know it's true. We all saw the way she acted when we found out the boys were tagging along this morning. Katie can't handle change. That's why she's so upset you're getting married."

Katie jumped to her feet. "I am not! I'm thrilled for Bree and Nathan. Just because I have a head squarely on my shoulders and a plan for life, you're all upset because we couldn't have a two-week trip instead of the one. Well, some of us have to work for a living. And some of us are ready to grow up."

"Grow up!" Skye threw her hands in the air. "Grow up! You keep saying that. If you mean ready to settle down to a dull life and the same routine every day, every week, then no. I'm not ready to grow up. I want to have fun and live a little. And I sure don't faint when I get around a bunch of boozies or complain when my friends find me a hot guy to hang out with."

Camden gripped the edge of the table, unsure what to do or if he should do anything at all. The hurt and anger chasing each other across Katie's face couldn't decide if they wanted to land. But things were going to implode if someone didn't step in.

"Skye, that's too far." Bree's voice wasn't raised, but it was strict.

"No. Bree, just leave it. Let her get away with this too." Katie pushed her chair in. "Thanks for dinner, Camden. It was great."

Her footfalls dashed up the stairs, and a door slammed.

"Going after her, Cam? Or are you just going to keep pretending like there's nothing between you two?" Ryan wadded up his napkin.

Camden realized he was on his feet too. "I thought I'd better do dishes."

"That's what I thought." Ryan picked up his plate and carried it to the kitchen. "I'll go check us into the hotel and be back to pick you up later. Or you can catch a ride if I don't get back when you're ready."

"Come on, Skye. Let's go walk for a while. We need to talk." Bree grabbed her friend's arm and dragged her towards the door. "You're welcome to stay as long as you need, Camden. Sorry to leave all the cleaning to you."

"It's a good way to work off the energy." He stacked plates, making sure he didn't slam them too forcefully. No need to break anything else tonight. Enough hearts had shattered already.

And as much as he wanted to go up and check on Katie, he'd give her time. No point in upsetting her more. If she wanted to talk, he'd be here waiting.

# 9

"Oh." Katie's voice behind him made him pause, but he didn't turn around. Might frighten her off. "I expected Bree to be here."

"She and Skye went for a walk." Camden set the last plate in the drainer.

"And you got stuck with the dishes?" She sounded nearer now.

"I chose to wash dishes. Gave me time to think." Camden drained the water and rinsed out the leftover soap. Slowly turned around.

"That was nice of you anyway. You shouldn't have had to do that after cooking too." She stood on the other side of the island, her head down, her fingers playing with the edge of the marshmallow bag. "What's this?"

"I had thought we might make s'mores, but ... well ..." He hung the towel over the oven handle and stepped to where only a counter separated them.

"Mmm." Her eyes raised just a bit, and he could see the puffiness where she'd been crying. "That sounds good."

"We still can, if you want." He wouldn't push her into anything. She'd already been pushed around by the girls she called friends tonight. "We could even make extras and just wrap them in foil for when the others get back."

"Okay." She opened the bag and popped one of the fluffy white confections in her mouth.

He grabbed a long serving fork and a couple bamboo skewers he found in a drawer. She'd already carried the ingredients into the living room and studied the fireplace. He turned the key to start the gas, then reached in and hit the igniter. It lit almost instantly, and a pretty blaze filled the space.

Sitting side by side on the hearth, they each held two marshmallows over the fire. Neither said anything or looked at the other. But it wasn't uncomfortable. She laughed as she pulled out a marshmallow with flame on the corner. A short puff, and the gooey treat was ready to go between the graham crackers. They worked as a team, making several extras for the others and then poking more marshmallows back into the fireplace to make their own.

She cooked two and ate one straight off the fork, not waiting for it to melt the chocolate. Although she licked her fingers clean, a little trail of white stickiness clung to the edge of her mouth. He reached over and used the pad of his thumb to catch it.

"Second night in a row you've caught me with something there." She ducked her head again, focused on mashing her s'more down where it was small enough to fit in her mouth. Was she remembering their almost-kiss from the last time? He couldn't get it off his mind, especially with the flames casting a glow over her.

She glanced up at him, then back into the fireplace. He swallowed and tried to focus too, but he couldn't concentrate on anything but her. Everything else was just a haze.

"Your marshmallow's on fire." She grabbed his hand and pulled it back, blowing the flame out before it could blacken any more of the sugary mess.

"Thanks." He quickly mashed it between the crackers and chocolate. A quick twist of the key, and the flame died down again. "Let's go walk. The sun should set in an hour or so."

She nodded and they finished their treats as they made their way out of the condo and down to the beach. There weren't many people around this evening, the rain having run most of them off. The waves crashed slightly farther out now. Shells and other items washed up during the storm rested on the sand. Without a word, they walked at the edge of the foamy water, not touching, but not far apart either.

A few joggers churned their way up the sand. A cool breeze dashed around them, knocking Katie's curls this way and that. Every so often, she'd pick up a sea creature and toss it into the water so it could ride back out to sea.

Singing drifted toward them from a group seated in a circle farther up the beach. He closed his eyes and listened, picking out the words of the familiar praise song. The message was that God was all around them, even in the foam of the ocean waves and the beauty of a sunset. The sky tonight blazed with pinks and purples and oranges, lighting up the leftover clouds and echoing in the reflection on the water. Yes. He could see God in that.

"You okay?" Katie's question brought him back to the present.

"Fine. Just enjoying the singing." He motioned to the group. "They'd probably let us join if we asked."

A look of near terror crossed her face.

"We don't have to."

She ducked her head, kicked her feet in the water that rushed over her toes for a moment before receding again. "It's not that I don't believe in God, Camden. I do. We don't always see eye to eye, but I believe in Him."

"I'm not sure what that means, but okay. And worshiping Him isn't something you like to do because you don't see eye to eye?"

"I just don't handle meeting new people easily."

"So, you want to work in an environment where you have to talk to strangers all day?" He wasn't making fun of her. Simply trying to understand.

"That's different, though. I don't have to get to know them. No more than to help them find a book or make sure their fines are paid." She glanced toward the worshipers. "But with a group like that, they'd want to know all about me. Where I'm from, how long I'm here, if I'm a Christian, how I came to God."

"And you're afraid I might hear." Camden tossed a shell into the ocean.

"No." She shook her head, turned to walk the other way. "It's not that. I'm ... I guess I'm very private. I don't open up easily. Bree probably didn't get me to really talk to her until we'd been rooming together for a whole semester."

"Are you as upset about her getting married as Skye thinks?" Camden regretted the question as soon as it left his mouth, but he'd been wondering the whole evening.

"Like Skye said, I don't handle change well." Katie's voice held frustration and hurt.

"And Bree's leaving you behind."

Katie stopped and stared at him.

"What? I know how colleges like Freed-Hardeman work." He pointed at her. "You go in expecting to find a boyfriend and get married either while you're there or just after. My cousin did."

"That works well for people who are extroverts like Bree

and Skye." Katie hugged herself. "Not as much for people who keep to themselves."

"The boys didn't try to get to know you simply because of how pretty you are?" He tugged her to a mostly dry piece of sand, and they sat, staring out at the sky's fading colors.

"You're kidding right?" She ran a hand through her hair.

"You don't think you're pretty?"

"I know I'm not. Skye has the looks guys want. Or Bree with her bubbly laughter and caring heart." Katie motioned a hand down the length of her body. "I'm just plain old Katie. No personality and no looks."

"You, with the wild curls that make me want to reach out and touch them? You with the hazel eyes that change color depending on your T-shirt and your mood? You with the legs that look like that? And your cute toes and nose and full lips?" Camden leaned as close as he dared. "You're gorgeous. Skye has nothing on you."

<hr>

Katie tried to catch her breath. Camden couldn't be serious. Could he? She wasn't gorgeous.

The wind blew a curl over her face and she reached up to move it, but his hands beat her to it. He ever so gently caressed it and then tucked it behind her ear. His finger ran down the length of her cheek, traced her jaw.

She turned her face quickly away. "You're not really attracted to me. Just the idea of me."

"Look, Katie." Camden waited a second and then reached over and turned her face back to him. "I'm scared too."

She searched his blue eyes. Intense. Serious. No joking around with him. Everything he said was the truth, whether she believed him or not.

Really?

"What are you scared of?" She squeezed her question out around a lump growing in her throat.

"I'm terrified of falling in love with another woman who isn't really interested in me."

She frowned. "Another woman?"

"I was engaged a few years ago." Camden's eyes turned toward the darkening ocean. "Jennifer. But a few weeks before our wedding, she called it off. Decided she wanted something different for her life. Or someone different, I guess I should say."

"Oh." Katie yearned to reach out and wrap him up, but fear held her in place.

"I thought I was okay. That I'd moved past it. That maybe I could eventually find someone else. Although I never dreamed I'd meet anyone on a vacation who intrigued me like you do. Just not the kind of thing that happens to me, you know?"

"I know." Boy, did she know. It wasn't the kind of thing that happened to her either.

"And like you keep saying, it can't be real, right?" Camden leaned back on his hands. "It's just a fairy tale dream we're living for a few days. You'll head off to somewhere else tomorrow. And if the way Skye and Ryan were acting tonight is any indicator, she won't tell him the next stop, so this is it. The end."

The end. So final. So sad. Not happy at all, as a fairy tale should be.

"You don't think Skye already told Ryan?" Katie leaned her elbows on her knees.

"He said she only let him know about this area. Promised to tell him more later if this worked out." Camden let out a long breath. "But the way things exploded at the dinner table tonight, I'm guessing that's not going to happen."

"It was a bit ... intense." Katie released a short laugh.

They sat in silence for several long minutes while stars lit the sky one by one. The singing down the beach stopped. Laughter and chatter replaced it. There weren't any more joggers. And they'd never come across Skye and Bree.

She wrestled with her brain. She'd been so excited when she landed the job at the library and found the perfect apartment only a few days later. Everything had worked out smoothly and without a hitch. Wasn't that more important than risking it all on a *what if?*

"I should probably walk you back. Maybe Ryan will come back and pick me up before long." Camden pushed to his feet and reached down to give her a hand.

The moonlight highlighted his sandy hair differently from the sunshine. His hands were strong and sure, warm and tender. She looked up at him as they stood only inches apart on the peaceful stretch of beach.

"If you get nothing more from all of this, I hope you get this." He cupped the side of her face. "You're beautiful. And any man would be a fool to not at least try to get to know you better with the hopes that maybe forever would come from it."

Her heart had somehow crept up to her throat. The pulse beat so strongly there, it must be obvious even in the dark. Could he hear the pounding that was stronger than the waves and faster than any normal heart should beat?

She didn't know a thing about this guy except for what he'd told her. And even that he could've made up.

And yet nothing he'd said came across as false or insincere. What if she took a chance on this? What if she decided to change the way her life was going? So what if he ended up living nowhere close? They could figure that out down the road, right?

She took a step closer, placed her hands on his chest, lifted her face. No friends around to interrupt this time. But she couldn't stop now. Even if this was just a dream, every fairy tale had at least one kiss. Why shouldn't she?

Weaving his hand through her curls, he clasped the base of her neck. The other wrapped around her waist and flattened against her back. His eyes searched hers as he lowered his face, one tiny half inch at a time. She raised up on her tiptoes and met him halfway, pressing her lips to his.

He froze for a second and then pulled her even closer, moving his mouth across hers, gently and sweetly. Her hands grabbed his shoulders. Then the back of his neck.

Breath fast, he pulled away just slightly, then wrapped her up with her head against his chest. His heart beat almost as hard as hers, the rhythm steady and strong under her ear. For a dream, this was the realest she'd ever felt.

His phone ringing shattered the moment into a million pieces. They both jerked away from each other, awkward, now that they no longer embraced. He pulled his cell from his pocket and swiped to answer it, one hand running through his hair.

"Hey." He pressed the device to his ear. "Yeah. I'm on the beach. Be there in a few minutes."

She wrapped her arms around her middle, trying to hold herself together. What now? What did that change? Anything? Nothing?

"Ryan's waiting for me in the parking lot of the condo." Camden scuffed a toe against the sand and shrugged. "Guess we'd better head that way before he leaves me."

"Right." Her voice sounded more normal than she'd expected.

They walked side by side as before, but this time when his hand brushed against hers, she caught his pinky in the crook of hers. He tugged her slightly closer. She resituated until all her fingers wove through his. And it felt right.

It shouldn't surprise her that God would set up something so wonderful only to take it away again. After all, He'd taken other things away from her in the past. And He took Camden's fiancée away too. Not that Katie could complain too much about that one.

Ryan flashed his lights as they walked into the parking lot. Camden held up a finger and turned her toward the door. In the shadowy entranceway, they paused. Had Skye and Bree come back already, or was Katie about to walk into an empty condo?

"I'm glad we got to know each other." He clung to her hands.

She couldn't blame him. She wasn't quite ready to let go either.

"Do you want my phone number? Just in case?"

That would put the ball in her court, and she wasn't always the bravest person in the world. She pulled her bottom lip through her teeth. Did she? But could she give him hers? What if he never called? That would hurt worse than saying goodbye right now and never seeing each other again.

"You don't have to." Camden's voice was low, quiet ... but pleading. "I just hoped."

She tugged a hand loose and pulled her phone out. With three swipes, it was unlocked and open to receive a new number. She pressed it into his hand, afraid to look at his face.

Two seconds later, he returned it. Was that enough time for him to have entered a number? She'd look later. She couldn't handle it right now.

"I better go. Ryan is in a mood tonight. I probably need to let him vent some before I'll be able to get any sleep."

She nodded. "We're headed out right after breakfast tomorrow too."

Hooking a thumb under her chin, he raised her face to his for one more feathery kiss. "Goodnight, Katie."

"Goodnight, Camden."

When Katie walked in, Bree was video chatting with Nathan. She waved from the couch but didn't move. Her expression was undecipherable, but it looked like trouble in paradise. Katie chose to go on upstairs, not wanting to witness any lovers' spat.

From the sounds of the other bedroom, Skye was taking advantage of the Jacuzzi tub. Katie laid back on the bed she'd share with Bree tonight. She opened her contacts and scrolled down to the *C*'s. No Camden. Had he changed his mind at the last minute?

Going back to the top, she scanned each and every entry to see if he'd put it under something different. Did he spell it with a *K*? No. In the *P's*, she froze and giggled. *Prince Charming*. The area code was 901. Why did that sound so familiar?

She'd look it up later. For now, she needed to calm the rest of the way down so she could get some sleep tonight. Tomorrow would be a long day, despite the pleasure of seeing her sister's family at the end of it.

Prince Charming. Her fairy tale come true. But would this story have a happily ever after? It was up to her now.

# 10

Katie inhaled deeply as she raised her hands above her head, pressing her left foot to her right thigh. Exhale. Inhale. Exhale.

The sun saluted her back, sending shards of pink and orange across the sky. The surf pounded the beach as it crept back in for the day. She lowered her foot and raised the other. Inhale. Exhale.

She slid her legs wide and flowed into a different pose, her right elbow on her left knee, her palms pressed together. Inhale. Exhale.

When she discovered yoga three years before, it had become her go-to for stress relief. She didn't practice the meditation aspect of it, but often used the time and deep breaths to focus on praying, offering her worries to God. If she could only remember to leave them there afterward.

She slid to the other side and repeated the position. The tension from the last few days practically sloughed off her, slid down her legs, and soaked into the sand under her mat. Inhale. Exhale.

"What should I do, God?" She pressed into the twist more to work a kink out of her back that had been there for a few days. "You know I like him, but we hardly know each other."

Just a couple more standing stretches and then she'd move to the ones where she sat. The beach was almost deserted this time of day. Most of the vacationers in the area would miss the sunrise, and that was a shame because this one just kept getting better.

"And I don't even know where he lives. I mean, he could be from Alaska or something. How would that work?" She sat with her legs stretched out in front of her and bent over to clasp her heels, pressing her forehead to her shins. It had taken her a while to work up the limberness to be able to bend all the way over, and she was proud of her elasticity. If only she could be so flexible in life situations, able to twist and flow with whatever came her way. But she remained brittle, as Skye had pointed out last night.

Lying back, she pulled a leg across her body, bending her knee. Inhale. Exhale.

"I know some people say You talk directly to them, showing them what You want for their lives. If You have any desire to do that for me, now would be a great time." She switched legs. "Because I'm seriously at a loss."

She sat up and crossed her legs, back straight, her hands relaxed on her knees. Inhale. Exhale.

The colors in the sky were fading, making way for the blue. A few joggers headed across the damp sand, listening to head-phones or running with a friend. Running had never been a good release for her. She drew in another deep breath and let it slowly out, emptying as much air from her lungs as possible.

In a few minutes, she'd have to get back and throw her last remaining items in her bag, but this was the most peace she'd enjoyed in days. A dream come true. She closed her eyes and took one more breath.

"Katie?"

Her eyes flew open, the air she'd just taken in stuck somewhere inside her throat.

Camden stood in front of her, sweat glistening on his forehead. He leaned over and rested his hands on his knees, his own breath coming in bursts. How had she missed that he was one of the runners? Though it didn't surprise her, considering how lean his body was.

"Good morning." Katie let the air leak from her lips.

"You're out early." Camden pulled the edge of his shirt up and wiped his face. She tore her eyes away from his toned chest. She'd already seen enough of it during the last few days.

"Fulfilling a dream." She unwound her legs and rose to her feet. "I always wanted to do yoga on the beach at sunrise."

"I wasn't sure what you were going to say, but I don't think that was it." He leaned down and touched one toe to stretch his own legs out.

"The video I used to use every day when I first started was set on a beach at sunrise. It always looked so peaceful. So, as soon as I knew we were going to stop here, I decided unless it was raining, I would do it." She shook her mat off to remove most of the sand.

"I guess you didn't strike me a yoga type." He straightened again. "You're out here by yourself?"

"I brought my pepper spray, just in case. And my phone." She put the bag with her mat over her shoulder. "And I'm not sure what the 'yoga type' is, I guess. I suppose I'm too nerdy?"

"Katie." He stepped closer, reached out then pulled back again. Did he regret what had happened last night? Was he wishing he hadn't given her his number?

She clasped her arms across her chest, trying to hide the

hurt. She turned and took a step away. "I guess I'll see you around then. Or not."

"Katie." He caught her arm this time, holding tightly but not painfully. "I didn't touch you just now because I'm all gross and I didn't think you'd want that. I don't think you're nerdy, and even if you were, I obviously think it's cute. And I was concerned about you being out here alone because I didn't want you to get hurt. That's all."

She wasn't quite ready to let herself turn around, but she did relax again. "Sorry. I guess I just wasn't sure if you were having regrets or not."

"No regrets." His clasp turned to a caress. "Never."

She finally turned. "Really?"

"Really."

The sand was cool where she dug her toe in. "I wasn't sure I'd even get to see you before we head out. But I figured Ryan probably coerced Skye into telling him where we're going."

Camden ran a hand over the back of his neck. "Actually, he didn't. So, needless to say I'm glad I caught you out here. Otherwise, last night would have been our goodbye."

"She didn't tell?" Katie frowned. This was it. The last time they'd be together unless she took advantage of having his number and called him.

"Evidently that's why he was so upset last night. He was mad because she wouldn't give away your next location." The pad of his thumb stroked circles on the edge of her arm.

"Huh." Katie pulled her bottom lip through her teeth. "I didn't even see her when I got in last night. She was locked in her room. And Bree was up late … chatting … with Nathan, so I didn't get a chance to talk with her either. And then, of course, I was up and out here before they got out of bed. They're actu-ally probably wondering where I am."

"Guess you better go." His fingers squeezed. "You said you

had a pretty long drive, right?"

She swallowed, tried to contain a smile that was creeping up over her lips.

"Katie?"

A giggle escaped her. "I'm sorry. I just had a crazy idea, and I'm not sure if I should act on it or not. It's so Skye-like. Not something I would do. And yet I want to!"

He looked in her eyes, concern written across his face. "Should I be worried?"

"It depends." She laughed again. "What are your plans for today?"

He shook his head. "Are you okay?"

She paused for a moment, considered everything. She'd asked God to give her a sign, and Camden had shown up less than ten minutes later. If she acted on her urge, this could buy her more time with him. More time to get to know him and even see what her sister thought. And possibly help her make up with Skye a bit too.

"I'm great." She stepped closer to him again, pressed a quick kiss to his mouth, and then whispered right in his ear, "We're going to Atlanta."

The deed done, she ran for it. But he was faster. He caught her at the edge of the beach, where the sea oats transitioned to pavement.

Camden clasped her fingers in his, afraid to let go. Had she really just done that? Kissed him in broad daylight and then given him his most desired information? Was this the same girl from the last few days? Was yoga magic?

"Atlanta, Georgia?"

She gave him a sheepish grin.

"You're kidding." He released a breathless laugh of his own.

"I'm not. We're staying with my sister."

"Jodie?"

"You remembered my sister's name?" She rocked back on her heels.

"I remember everything you've told me over the last three days." He gave her a tug. "Good grief. Atlanta."

"Why is that making you laugh?" That cute little wrinkle in her forehead was back again.

"That's where Uncle John lives. We were probably heading that way today anyway."

Her mouth hung open. "No way."

"Seriously." Camden guffawed. "Ryan and I talked about it last night. He didn't want to go home but then remembered his dad has tickets to the game tonight. He figured if nothing else, that would be more fun than hanging here another day without you girls."

"The game tonight?" She gave his shoulder a little push. "The Braves game?"

"Of course. My uncle has season tickets. He keeps a box and uses it for a lot of his business associates."

"A box?" Her voice had risen an octave. "Oh my goodness! Box seats to the Braves?"

"I take it you're a fan?" Who was this girl?

"You could say that." She looked to be trying to compose herself but still had a little bounce in her toes. Her phone rang and she jumped. "Oops! I bet Bree's wondering what's taking me so long."

He waited while she promised her friend she'd be there in just a few minutes.

"You better get back. Want me to walk you?" Even knowing they were heading in the same direction he didn't want to let her go again yet. After all, Atlanta was a big city.

"No."

His heart skipped a beat.

"Listen. What if you go back and get ready to go, too, and I'll text you more information?"

His pulse picked up again.

"Maybe we can meet up at the next rest area down the road? How long do you think it'll take you guys to get ready to leave?"

"Less than an hour for sure."

She wanted to make this work. She was going to use the number he'd given her. No matter what else happened today, it couldn't get better.

"Okay. I'll text you if I find out that plan won't work, but I'll definitely find a way for us to meet up again in the city. We'll be over near Stone Mountain. That's our plan for tomorrow." She turned to go, but he pulled her back one more time.

"You're not just trying to get tickets to the game tonight, are you?" He crooked a grin at her.

"No!" Righteous indignation flashed on her face until she realized he was teasing. "Although it would be icing on the cake!"

"I'll see what I can do." He laughed again. "If I wasn't all sweaty, I'd pull you to me for a proper kiss."

She stepped closer again and leaned her face up. He ran a finger down her cheek and then pressed his lips against hers, relishing the feel of her skin under his, the softness of the curls tickling his fingers, the way her breath caught when he deepened it for a moment.

"You're nothing like I thought you'd be when I fished you out of the pool earlier this week." He kissed her forehead. "You're so much more."

She squeezed his hands and backed up as her phone dinged again. "They'll come looking for me if I don't go."

"Go on. I'll watch for the text." He stared after her until she turned the corner to head behind the condo. Then he picked up his feet and huffed it back to their hotel. He needed a shower before he saw her again. Because next time, he didn't want that much space between them.

Was this real? Wasn't it less than twenty-four hours before he'd given the whole thing up as a lost cause, thinking she wasn't much different from Jennifer? He was so wrong. Katie was amazing.

"You're grinning like a fool." Ryan lounged on the bed, the weather channel blaring on the television set.

"I may be a fool, but I'm a happy one. Get up and get ready to go. We need to be ready in less than an hour if we want to catch them." Camden stepped into the bathroom and flipped the faucet to start the water heating up.

"Catch them?" Ryan pushed the door open. "The girls?"

"You did want to, right?" Camden pulled off his sweaty shirt.

"You know where they're going?"

"I know where they're going." Camden pulled the shower curtain and started scrubbing.

"How?"

"Let's just say I'm not at odds with them like you are." Camden hummed as he shampooed his hair.

He showered in peace for a few moments, and then Ryan's voice was back. "Did you kiss her?"

"What?" He turned the water off.

"You kissed her, didn't you?"

Camden pulled his towel behind the curtain with him and dried off. "Why do you think I kissed someone?"

"I saw how close you were with Katie last night when you finally came back to the condo." Ryan stood with his arms crossed, leaning against the counter. "You thawed the ice queen?"

"She's not an ice queen." Camden quickly pulled on clean clothes and gathered the few belongings scattered around the rest of the room. "But yes. We kissed. Because we both felt the attraction, and because we're trying to get to know each other a little in the time we have together."

"And so she told you where they're going?"

"Are you packed?" Camden zipped his duffle bag. "You're never going to get over it when you hear their destination."

"Florida?" Ryan threw a few things in his suitcase.

"Atlanta!"

Ryan's face was priceless. "What are we waiting for?"

Camden's phone dinged. "This."

I'm so glad we ran into each other this morning, PC. We're leaving in about ten minutes. Stopping at the first rest area on I-65. See you soon.

*PC?* He smiled as he realized she'd adopted the nickname he'd given himself. He could handle being considered a Prince Charming.

PS—I wonder, if you're Prince Charming, which princess am I?

Her second text made him laugh again. He was doing that a lot this morning.

"Well?" Ryan stood at the door, arms crossed.

"Let's roll. We'll catch them at the rest area on I-65."

"Because that worked so well last time." Ryan's muttered complaints behind him couldn't shake the smile from Camden's face. He was too busy chasing his happily ever after. Nothing could upset him.

# 11

"Are you for real?" Skye's question made Katie giggle.

Camden leaned against the hood of Ryan's car, watching the girls as they headed down the sidewalk from the restroom. Skye and Bree threw a shocked glance over their shoulders at her. Katie grinned sheepishly.

"How did you find us? Did you follow us?" Skye put her hands on her hips and stopped right in front of Ryan. "I told you not to."

"Not my idea this time." Ryan hooked his thumb over at Camden.

"You followed us?" Bree turned to Katie. "Katie, I'm so sorry we encouraged you to get closer to this guy."

"Bree, I told him." A frisson of unease rippled through her belly. Wasn't this a good idea? Hadn't Bree encouraged this?

Bree blinked. A wary look passed over her face.

Camden straightened. "Besides, we were headed to Atlanta today anyway."

"What?" Skye looked back and forth between everyone, obviously unsure what was going on.

"Ryan's from Atlanta. His dad promised to let him use his season tickets at the game tonight if we came back a day early." Camden crossed his arms. "When Katie let it slip that you were headed this way, too, we worked it out to meet up here."

"Katie?" Skye looked stunned.

"Call your sister right now." Bree poked Katie in the arm.

"What? Why?" Katie took a step back.

"I want you to explain this to her before we arrive on her doorstep with two strangers in tow." Bree reached into Skye's car and pulled out Katie's cell. "Call her."

"Bree, be serious. I'll explain when we get there." Katie didn't take the phone.

Katie had expected Skye and Bree to be thrilled. Instead, it was like they were living a repeat of yesterday, only with swapped roles. What had gotten into Bree?

Bree ran her fingers across the screen and handed it back to Katie. "Too late."

"You dialed her number?" Katie caught the phone before it hit the pavement and quickly put it to her ear, shooting her friend a dirty look. "Hey Jodie."

"Hey, sis. Everything okay? Still going to be here before dinner?" Jodie's voice held no concern.

"Yep. We left on schedule. Bree just wanted me to tell you something before we get there." Katie walked toward an area of picnic tables.

"What did you do?" Jodie's voice teased. "You didn't get a tattoo or anything, did you? Because I'm so not helping you defend that to Mom."

"No, nothing like that." Katie rolled her eyes. "She just wanted me to give you a heads up. You see, we met some guys ..."

"Guys? Katie, you didn't elope, did you?"

"Will you quit jumping to conclusions?" Katie tugged on

one of her curls. "No. I'm not married. But we've been hanging out with these guys the last few days, and they happen to be headed to Atlanta too—"

"Do you know anything about them? Are they Christians? Where do they live? Are they following you? Do I need to have the police here when you arrive?"

Katie held the phone away from her ear for a second and let out a frustrated growl. "No. Jodie, stop it. They're just guys. Fun to hang out with, sweet and nice. Yes. Camden is a Christian. No. You do not need to call the police. I'm going to hang up now before you get even more crazy. We'll see you this afternoon."

"Katie!" Jodie's voice caught her before she could end the call.

"What?"

"I'm sorry. I just want to make sure you're okay. You're the only sister I have."

"I know. I'm sorry for the short notice, but I really think you'll approve."

"Okay. I'll look forward to your visit even more, then. Drive safe, okay?" Jodie blew a kiss through the phone. "And maybe send me a picture?"

Katie rolled her eyes. "Or not."

But she held the phone up on selfie mode to see if she could discreetly snap a shot of him over her shoulder for her snoopy older sibling. When his nose was all she saw in the screen, she jumped and spun around. He stood right behind her, one eyebrow raised.

"I thought you said she didn't have to call the police? I take it she wanted a picture to search through the wanted posters?" His smirk told her he was teasing more than the lilt of his voice.

"She's just nosy, actually." Katie clasped the device to her chest.

"Here." Camden snatched it from her hand and leaned over to where their faces were right next to each other. "Smile."

She barely got the corners of her mouth turned up before he snapped the picture. Then, he took another one while pressing a kiss to her cheek. She gasped and peeked over her shoulder to see if the others had seen. No one seemed to be looking their way.

"Camden, seriously." She snatched her cell back and swiped to see the results. The first one wasn't bad, but the second one was comical at best, with her wide eyes and open mouth.

"Definitely a keeper. You should send her that one."

"That would be a big fat *no*." Katie texted her the first one, though. It was a good shot of him, regardless of what she'd looked like. And it wasn't like Jodie wouldn't see him this evening. "Think Bree and Skye are okay with this? They didn't act very happy to see you guys."

"I think they were more concerned that it would upset you again." Camden ran a finger down her cheek. "Maybe having talked to your sister will help Bree accept it better."

"Here's hoping."

Bree looked up as Katie and Camden rejoined their group.

"Everyone good to go now?" Katie made her smile as large as possible.

"Are we?" Bree asked, lifting one eyebrow.

"I am. Jodie's looking forward to seeing us. And we're losing an hour when we hit Georgia, so let's quit wasting daylight, people." Katie clapped.

"Well, okay then." Skye tossed the keys to Katie. "Your turn to drive."

"See you in a bit." Camden's whisper in her ear sent a

shiver down her back. She couldn't squelch the grin that crept over her mouth.

"Spill it." Bree's voice sent off a vibe that would harbor no nonsense.

"So, I did what you guys wanted me to and got to know Camden a bit better last night. We took a walk on the beach, talked about God and fears."

"And?" Skye leaned forward in the backseat. "Did he kiss you?"

Katie clamped her lips together, but it was too late. Her face gave her away. Skye squealed and Bree slapped her arm.

"You didn't say a thing when you came in last night. Or this morning."

"You were talking to Nathan last night." Katie glanced at her friend and then back to the road. "And this morning, I had just come back from running into him on the beach. He'd been out running and found me at the end of my yoga routine."

"And you decided to tell him where we were going, just like that?" Skye snapped. "That is so not like you. Maybe I'm a good influence."

"Or a bad one." Bree frowned at their bubbly friend. "Katie, are you sure about this? You were so set against it yesterday morning."

"And then you pushed me to make up with him. And we spent all day together. And I'd been praying this morning for God to tell me whether or not I should pursue this. Then, he showed up not ten minutes later. Don't you think maybe God was saying, 'okay'?"

"You're going to blame us if this doesn't work out, aren't you?" Bree leaned back in her seat.

"What?" Katie hit the steering wheel with the heel of her hand. "Bree, seriously. Did you and Nathan fight or something? Because you're confusing me. For two days you encouraged me to give this a chance, and now you're telling me it doesn't have one?"

"Yeah, Bree. What gives?"

"I wouldn't call it a fight." Bree crossed her arms and looked out the window. "But he did tell me that he wasn't sure we'd been making the wisest choices when it came to these guys. And that he wished he'd put his foot down a little harder and insisted I not come on this trip."

Katie reached over and gave her hand a squeeze. "Was he jealous?"

"I don't know." Bree swiped at a tear. "Maybe. But I assured him the guys were interested in the two of you and not me. And that I had no interest in anyone but him. Anyway, he was relieved when he found out I'd convinced Skye not to tell our next stop because then we wouldn't have to worry about them anymore."

"And now you're afraid he's going to be mad." Katie pursed her lips. She hadn't meant to hurt her friend's relationship with her fiancé. "I can call Camden and tell him we'll just try texting and calling after our vacation is over. I don't need to go to the Braves game with him tonight. Although, considering how my phone is blowing up, I'd say Jodie might still want to meet him."

"The Braves game?" Skye leaned forward again. "He's taking you to the Braves game?"

"He said his uncle had a box and season tickets. Offered to call and see if we could use them."

"You and your baseball." Bree laughed, wiping away the leftover moisture. "Maybe I should have you call Nathan. If you explain that baseball's involved, he'll understand better."

"Here. See what Jodie is saying." Katie handed her phone to Bree.

"She says, in all caps, 'OH, HE'S CUTE!' and then has about

a million emojis behind it with hearts and smiles." Bree giggled. "Want to hear your other text message?"

"What?" Katie glanced over, but Bree was hiding the screen from her. "Who's it from?"

"Someone named Prince Charming?" Bree waved the phone in the air.

"Bree!" Katie reached for it, but Bree kept it too far away. "You can put it down now. I'll look at it later."

"I already saw it. Sure you don't want to know what it says?"

Katie let out a huff of air. "What does it say?"

"He doesn't think you're Cinderella."

"What does that mean?" Skye poked Katie in the shoulder.

Katie smiled. Camden had been thinking about her earlier text, wondering which princess she was to his Prince Charming. But the girls didn't need to know that yet. For now, she was just going to enjoy the thrill of this ride.

"Oh guys, look!" Skye pointed to a billboard advertising Six Flags.

"We're not going to ride roller coasters. We agreed to go check out Stone Mountain tomorrow." Bree shook her head.

"I know. I know. But man. I haven't gone to an amusement park in ages." Skye leaned back.

"Jodie's house is much closer to Stone Mountain than Six Flags. It's over on the other side of the city." Katie drew an imaginary map in the air.

"Sort of like a certain baseball stadium?" Bree's voice held sarcasm.

"If Jodie would rather I stay with her tonight, I will. After all, that's one of the reasons we chose to come this way." Katie nodded to emphasize her point. "There will always be opportunities in the future for going to see a baseball game."

"What about Camden?" Bree gave her a sharp glance.

"What about him?"

"What if he wants to go to the game anyway?"

"It's up to him." Katie shrugged. "This is our girls' trip. I have his number now and can get to know him better another time."

"Who are you and what have you done with my level-headed friend who doesn't take risks?" Bree playfully swatted her.

"I'm still me." Katie grinned. "I just found out that it's sort of fun to live in a fairy tale sometimes."

"You and your story references." Skye huffed in the backseat.

Camden understood them. That's all that mattered. Although she really did hope Jodie approved when they met in person. And agreed that a baseball game was just what they needed.

Camden played with his cell phone, turning it over and over in his hands. Katie hadn't replied to his message, but she'd been driving when he sent it, and they hadn't had any privacy when they stopped for lunch. Maybe they could talk about it later. Or he'd send another message tonight. He liked the thought of continuing the flirtation for a while longer.

"So, you're over Jennifer now?" Ryan glanced over from behind the steering wheel as they followed Skye's convertible through traffic.

"I think I've been over her for a while and just hadn't admitted it." Camden picked at a spot of dirt on his jeans. "I mean, it's been two years."

"Yeah, but yesterday you were still uptight about it. To the point that you wouldn't even let me say her name." Ryan shook his head. "And I thought you were the kind of guy who moved slow and didn't jump into things. Isn't that what you're always getting on to me for?"

"I'm not moving that fast."

"You're meeting some of her family." Ryan hit the turn signal to tail Skye off the interstate. "And you've only known her a few days."

"So? I'm not proposing marriage or anything." Camden folded his arms across his chest.

"Just using your family connections to impress her with a Braves game." Ryan smirked.

"That just sort of happened. I mentioned it, and you should have seen her face light up." Camden smiled. "I've never seen anyone get that excited about baseball."

"A girl who likes sports. Obviously, I have been focusing on the wrong friend." Ryan snickered and glanced around as they headed down a street full of houses.

"Ha. Don't even try to do anything about it now." Camden shot his cousin a warning look and then wiped his sweaty palms on his legs. He might have played it cool a moment ago, but meeting Katie's sister was a big deal to him. Katie seemed close to her. Maybe if he could impress the sibling, he'd eradicate that last bit of doubt hanging around Katie.

Ryan parked on the street in front of a one-story brick house. A handicap-capable minivan sat in the driveway next to the sloped yard, and a ramp ran down to the sidewalk from the small porch. In the front window, a little boy jumped up and down, banging his hands on the glass.

After racing up to the stoop, Katie pressed a kiss to the face on the other side of the panes. The door opened, and the boy leaped into Katie's arms, giggling as she spun him around and blew raspberries into his cheeks. Bree and Skye waited on the sidewalk and waved as a woman in a wheelchair came onto the stoop. A wheelchair?

Katie leaned down to give the woman a hug. Then she turned and pointed down toward him and Ryan. Ryan tugged on Camden's sleeve and pulled him up the walk. Katie beamed at him as he came up onto the porch with her.

"Jodie, this is Camden."

"It's nice to meet you, Jodie." Camden held out his hand, trying to remember if Katie had mentioned anything about her sister being disabled.

Jodie smirked up at him. "I can see Katie didn't warn you."

"I'm so sorry." Camden covered his eyes with his hand for a moment. "I just wasn't expecting ..."

"I know. But it's not that bad." Jodie patted the armrest of her chair. "Come on in. I think Riley is probably showing the others his cars. This could take a while."

Katie tugged his fingers as they walked through the door. She shot him a look of concern, but he smiled at her. The great first impression he'd set out to make had fallen way short, but maybe he could make it up now that he was past the shock.

"So, Camden." Jodie led them into a small but well-laid-out kitchen. "Katie tells me you've only known each other a few days."

"Oh, boy. Here comes in the inquisition." Katie muttered under her breath.

"We met her first night in New Orleans." Camden accepted the water Jodie handed him. "Thanks."

"Is that where you're from?" Funny that Jodie would ask a question her sister hadn't during the last three days.

"No. I live in Tennessee." Camden took a swig of water.

"Well, Katie, that's good news for you since you'll be living in same state now." Jodie smirked. "Unless you've changed your mind about working for the Germantown library?"

Germantown? Camden swallowed a shout of exultation. Instead, he threw up a *thank you* to God.

"Of course I haven't changed my mind." Katie frowned. "Why would I? It was a huge honor for them to offer me that position right out of school."

"I just wondered, now that you'd met Camden here."

"Jodie, you're ridiculous." Katie scooted a dining chair out and slid down to look right in her sister's eyes. "But it's a really good thing I met Camden, and you're going to think so too."

"Oh, am I?" Jodie glanced over at him and then turned back to her sister. "And why is that?"

"Because his uncle has tickets to a suite for the Braves game tonight." Katie's voice was almost more squeal than speech.

Camden covered his laughter with another drink of water.

"And his uncle having tickets means what for us?" Jodie frowned at her sister.

"It means we can go, silly!" Katie bounced and then seemed to remember herself. "But only if it's okay with you."

"I imagine he probably doesn't want your sister to tag along. He invited you." Jodie poked Katie in the arm.

"You're more than welcome too. I just need to let my uncle know the final headcount, and he'll send the electronic tickets to my phone." Camden held up a hand. "But I also know it's last minute. So, no obligation on your part."

"As much as Nick and I love baseball, I think we'll pass this time." Jodie squeezed her sister's hand to quiet her. "Riley gets really grumpy when he doesn't get to bed on time. And there's no way he'd get to sleep before midnight if he went to something so exciting. Plus, it's almost an hour from here."

Katie's shoulders slumped.

"Y'all should go, though." Jodie chucked Katie under the

chin. "But Katie, can you handle it? I mean, there's a lot of … drinking at baseball games."

Drinking? Camden frowned, wondering what Jodie was asking. Did this have anything to do with the way Katie had reacted Monday night?

"We'll be in a suite." Katie's eyes glanced to Jodie's legs and then back up again. "So, I won't be around much of it at all."

"I promise to keep her safe." Camden stepped forward and put a hand on Katie's other shoulder.

"I believe you." Jodie nodded to him. "And I hope we can spend more time together tomorrow. Because I'd love to hear how this all came about."

Looked like Katie's sister trusted him. That was a huge step toward approval, right? He'd take each and every one he could get.

# 12

"This place is amazing." Katie's fingers squeezed Camden's arm as they walked through the area around the ballpark.

Shops and restaurants lined the sidewalk with people finishing dinner, milling about, or following the rest of the crowd toward the stadium. Skye, Ryan, and Bree trailed along behind them with Skye exclaiming every now and then over something she'd seen in a window. Camden didn't envy his cousin having to steer that shopaholic through this mayhem.

"Oh, look!" Katie pointed toward the drumline, beating out their rhythm closer to the entrance.

Several danced and grooved to the music as the crowd surrounded the group of men. Katie stood entranced, and Camden soaked up her excitement. The stadium had only been open a few years, and it held a party atmosphere he'd seen in no other baseball arena. They paused again so Katie and the girls could watch the fountain dance. Several children played in the shooting streams, laughing as the water disappeared and then soared skyward again.

"We should have worn our swimsuits." Skye laughed.

In Camden's opinion, the girl wasn't wearing much more than that now. Katie's Braves T-shirt and khaki Bermudas were much more flattering than Skye's tank top and short shorts. He quickly turned his eyes away from Skye's bare shoulders and back to the girl who intrigued him more with her modesty and charm.

"Ready to go in now?" Camden leaned close to Katie so she could hear him. There was that scent again. Floral, but not overpowering.

She nodded, and they made their way through the ticket process, allowing the girls' bags to be searched.

"We'll need to go up and that way to get to the suite." Ryan pointed.

"Let's get a hot dog first." Katie indicated a restaurant. "There's nothing like a ballpark hot dog."

"You know we can order food in the suite, right?" Camden didn't stop her but shook his head.

"But it probably won't be the same." Katie stepped up to the counter and told the man what she wanted.

He grinned as she lifted the sausage to her nose and inhaled. If the only side of this girl he'd seen had been the one in New Orleans, he still would have been attracted to her. But this? This was a side of her that almost made him want to propose right away without getting to know her more. She seemed to soak up everything around them and relish it.

The hallway outside the suites was quieter, with only a few people walking around. As Camden pushed into the room and waved his hand around, the girls *oohed* and *aahed*. Ryan flopped down on a sofa against the wall and propped his feet up.

"Check this out." Camden pulled Katie across to the glass wall and motioned out to the field below.

"Oh." She studied the seats just outside the windows. "We can sit there?"

"Why would you when it's air conditioned in here?" Ryan crossed his arms behind his head. "Isn't this the point of having a suite at a ballpark?"

Katie shook her head. "If I wanted to watch the game on a television screen from an air-conditioned room, I'd have stayed at Jodie's. Besides, you can't join in the chop if you're in here."

"The chop?" Skye looked confused.

"When you move your arm like you're swinging a tomahawk." Ryan rolled his eyes. "Don't you watch baseball?"

"Only when I'm invited by someone else. And even then, I'm mostly here for my friends. I could care less about the game."

"Well, I'm headed out there." Katie pointed through the window.

Camden opened the door and Katie followed him onto the balcony. He secretly agreed. He loved coming out here and being closer to the experience. They leaned against the rail and studied everything around them. The only thing better than this would be tickets behind home plate. Maybe someday. If he did, he hoped Katie would be by his side. After having her here today, any other option seemed flat.

"I think you've ruined me for life. My dad is never going to believe this." She sank down into a chair and took a big bite of her hot dog. "Oh, man. This is so good."

Camden laughed and slid into the seat next to her. "How on earth did you become such a big baseball fan?"

"I don't have a brother. It's just Jodie and me. So, Dad would pull us up on his lap while he watched the games. He'd move my arm to do the chop. And I made sure to cheer whenever he did because it made him smile." She grinned. "As I got older, I decided to learn as much as I could because it was something special for just Dad and me. Jodie enjoyed it some, but never as much as I did."

"That's really neat you have baseball to share with your dad." Camden squeezed her hand. "I've never known a girl to be so excited over anything to do with sports."

Katie laughed. "Yeah. You're sort of making a dream come true today."

"That's what Prince Charming is supposed to do, right?" He smiled at her, and she laughed.

The others came out and stood with them for the National Anthem. Then they went back into the climate-controlled room, and Camden and Katie had the balcony to themselves. She leaned forward in her seat, jumping when a ball was hit hard. He ended up watching her more than the game.

After the fifth inning, Katie leaned back with slumped shoulders as the opposing team made another out. "They're really struggling tonight."

"Lots of bloopers." Camden nodded. "Are you giving up, then?"

"No way." Katie shook her head. "It's just frustrating when I know they're a really good team. But they're being sloppy, making mistakes. And that ump needs his eyes checked."

Camden chuckled. "Have you figured out which princess you are yet?"

She turned her attention to him for the first time since they'd sat down. "I haven't really given it much thought. Too busy trying to figure out Prince Charming."

"I'm not even sure I can name all the princesses." He scratched his head. "Who's your favorite?"

"Beauty." She waved her hand around. "I mean, she has the whole book-loving thing going on. And what librarian wouldn't fall in love with someone with a library like that?"

"But that would make me ... the beast?" He gave a mock frown.

"Hmm. This does have potential, doesn't it?" Her eyes sparkled with laughter as she grinned at him.

"Hey!" He leaned away. "Are you calling me grouchy and conceited?"

"That first night you came across a bit conceited." She twisted her lips off to one side. "I mean, you expected me to be some damsel in distress simply because I'd gotten knocked into the pool. And then assumed I wanted to ride around in a carriage with you, despite the fact that we'd just met."

"And here I thought I was charming and resourceful." He put on a fake pout. How much of what she'd just said had been teasing, and how much was what she really thought? Had he truly come across as high and mighty?

"You're very charming." She snuggled up to his arm and laid her head on his shoulder. "And I'm not just saying that because you got me into a Braves game."

Things picked up again in the sixth inning with the first baseman hitting a grand slam and tying the score. Camden thought for a moment he might have to tie a rope around Katie to keep her from falling. She jumped up and down, screaming and clapping, leaning half over the edge.

Bree stepped out and shook her head. "Katie, you're going to kill yourself."

Katie shot a grin over her shoulder and then joined in the chop that echoed through the stadium, her tanned arm pumping up and down to the rhythm. She practically danced back to her seat. He settled his arm over her shoulders and pulled her into a hug.

"Oh, let me take y'all's picture." Bree stepped down to the edge and held her phone up. "Say cheese!"

Camden smiled at the camera. How could he not smile?

This was one of the best nights of his life. And considering the one before, that was saying something.

———

The feel of Camden's arm across Katie's shoulders was bliss. His fingers played with the bottom of her shirt sleeve and sent goosebumps up her arm. It wasn't cold by any stretch of the imagination ... not in late May in Atlanta. But the breeze kept things comfortable enough that having him so close was more than nice.

Bree had gone back inside with the others, the seventh-inning stretch was over, and they were on the downhill side of the ballgame. She wasn't ready for it to end. If she'd been asked what a perfect date would be, this would have hit the nail right on the head. Any dates she went on from here on out would be dreary compared to this experience.

Would she ever get to date Camden again? Her heart squeezed at the thought. She didn't even know where he lived, besides Tennessee, and it was a very long state. And he hadn't said anything when her sister dropped her new hometown in their earlier conversation. Did that mean he didn't live close?

Now that she knew he was from Tennessee, his area code made more sense. The same one as the library—only a digit different from the one she'd had the last four years in Henderson. But with cell phones, an area code no longer meant a person still lived there. Her dad had one from Texas despite having lived in Alabama the last ten years.

She groaned as the other team snagged two more runs in the top of the eighth. "Come on, guys! Don't give this away now when we're so close."

Camden was laughing at her, but she didn't care. Ten

minutes later, the Braves scored three, and she breathed a bit easier. Just one more inning.

The realization that the night was almost over ruined her joy over the score. Atlanta was huge, and Ryan's house wasn't close to Jodie's. They'd brought separate cars tonight because of that fact. What was the likelihood of seeing Camden one more time before they headed home Saturday? Slim to none. That's what it was.

"You okay?" Camden's voice right next to her ear pulled her from her depression for a second. Instead of dwelling on the future, she needed to keep soaking up the now.

"Just sad it's almost over." She propped her feet up on the balcony edge.

"Unless they go to extra innings."

"There's a happy idea. The longer I can stay here with you, the better." She covered his hand with hers and gave a squeeze.

"I'm glad you feel that way." He pressed a kiss to her temple. "I feel exactly the same."

Their wish looked more and more possible. Two runs came in for the other team in the top of the ninth. Katie stood and leaned forward, her arms on the edge of the railing. There was no way she could sit down until her boys scored at least one more run. Two would be better, because they'd win. But one would be okay. That would give her and Camden the hoped-for extra innings.

"Katie." Bree stood in the glass doorway. "Ryan suggested we might be able to get out a little easier and avoid some of the traffic if we leave now instead of waiting until the end. I know you love this, but I was thinking that might help you avoid ... well, some of the other fans."

Was Bree kidding her? "Bree, I can't leave. We're down by one in the bottom of the ninth."

"Katie, remember what happened Monday night?" The

concern in Bree's voice brought Katie's head around from where she'd been watching the field. "There will be some of that going on down below too."

Bree was afraid she'd pass out again. And she might. She glanced at Camden, who studied her. Had he figured out what was wrong with her? Was he going to agree with Bree and cut their time together short?

*Crack!*

Katie spun around to see a ball flying toward the outfield. "Go ball, go!"

One of the outfielders churned up the dirt in right field as the ball landed in the upper deck. Katie lifted her hands and screamed. They'd done it. They were tied again. But Bree wanted to leave now without knowing if they went to extra innings or pulled it out in this one. And that would mean less time with Camden.

"Katie?" Bree touched her arm. "Now that you know it's tied, can we go?"

"I can't, Bree." Katie couldn't explain it here, not in front of Camden. But she couldn't give up any second she was allowed to spend by his side.

"Will you be okay?" Bree's eyes searched hers.

"I'll make myself be okay." Katie couldn't let a repeat of Monday night happen.

"Okay."

Boos echoed around the stadium as the ump called a third strike on the man batting. They had only one out left before extra innings. Katie chewed her bottom lip and focused on the game.

"You know this is probably our last night together for a while." Camden stood close enough that his hip bumped into her.

"I know." Her voice was barely louder than a whisper, but

he was close enough to hear it. "I guess it's too far for you guys to hang out tomorrow. I always forget just how big this city is."

"Yeah. I think Uncle John wants Ryan to stay home for a few days now. He's not thrilled with how this week went." Camden tapped his fingers on the edge.

Another out. On to the tenth inning. A few more stolen minutes with this man, but at what cost?

"Was he upset with you? I know you were supposed to be a voice of reason." Katie studied Camden's profile, admiring the sharp angles of his nose, the defined jawline, the way the edge of his mouth quirked up as he thought about her question.

"He wasn't elated, but he also knows his son well enough to know I did the best I could." Camden slid his arm around her shoulders again. "You're doing Stone Mountain tomorrow, right?"

"That's the plan, though I don't think Skye's thrilled with it. She's not much of an outdoorsy type."

"I wouldn't have pegged her as one." Camden laughed. "But you definitely need to spend time with your friends. And your sister. And we have each other's number now. We'll touch base once you're home again."

"Will I ever see you again?" She didn't even look to find out whatever had started everyone cheering. She needed to see his eyes as he answered.

"We will if I have my way." His voice was husky and full of promises that seemed too deep to believe.

Fireworks exploded to her right, and when she looked down, the Braves had scored one more run in the bottom of the tenth to pull out the win. Camden pressed a quick kiss to her forehead, and then they walked back up the stairs to the suite. She shivered at the air conditioning as she joined the rest of their group. Or had the uncertainty of how long it might be before she saw Camden again caused the shiver?

"Ready to weave through the throngs?" Ryan led the way.

Bree pressed in close on Katie's right, and Camden kept his arm around her waist from the other side. The party atmosphere that had filled the stadium before was three times wilder now. People walked around with half-drunk beers in their hands, some with bottles. The yeasty smell triggered Katie's gag reflex, and she covered her mouth and nose to try and block some of it.

"You okay?" Camden asked right in her ear.

She nodded and focused on following Ryan. The pounding in her ears picked up speed. Were all these people about to be on the road with her? What had she been thinking? Jodie warned her. So did Bree. But she'd just had to spend a few more minutes with Camden.

*I can do this.* She took a deep breath through her nose and squeezed Bree's hand until she was sure it was painful. Camden's arm tightened around her as he steered her around some people who were obviously several cups into the night. *Please don't let them be driving.* She closed her eyes and then opened them again. Almost out of the stadium. Maybe the smell wouldn't be so intense out in the open air.

The design of the area around the stadium didn't leave much room to spread out. They kept up as quick a pace as they could, but with thousands of people leaving at the same time, there wasn't much way to move any faster than a normal walk. A man walking toward them laughed loudly and threw out his arm as he passed. Golden liquid sloshed as if in slow motion and plopped onto Katie's shirt.

Her knees wobbled and went weak as the smell clung to her, the coldness of the beer seeping through to her skin. Camden was the only thing that held her up. Bree helped them move over to the side of the path.

"Katie?" Camden's eyes searched hers. "Katie, stay with me."

"Did it get on you?" Bree tugged at the fabric on Katie's torso. "We can go in here and change shirts, okay?"

"What's wrong, Katie?" Camden's voice held worry and a little panic.

"I told you." Bree's hiss came out harsher than she probably intended, and Katie grimaced. "It's the alcohol. She can't be around it."

"Is she allergic?" Camden clutched Katie's body to his as if he could shield her from everything around them.

"No." Bree shook her head. "It's ... it's just something she can't deal with. The best thing for us to do is to get her out of here as quickly as possible. There won't be as much in the parking garage because most of the drinkers will catch a ride from here."

The words strengthened Katie. They wouldn't all be driving.

She hated that Camden had seen her like this again. Why couldn't she control herself? Why couldn't she handle things like a normal person? Jodie never had this problem, and she'd suffered far worse than Katie had. Camden steered her back into the flow of traffic. Soon the crowd thinned as people headed to various parking spots.

"Feeling better?" Camden's lips brushed against her hair.

She nodded, unwilling to look up and see the pity or disgust in his face. Would he be put off by this? Twice in one week. She couldn't even stand herself right now.

Over by his car, Skye and Ryan whispered. Had they gotten closer like she and Camden had over the last few days? Katie hadn't even thought about asking Skye what was going on with Ryan. She'd just assumed it was a flirty fling because that's what Skye always had.

Camden pulled Katie over to the other side of Skye's car, where the others couldn't see as much. "Are you sure you're okay?"

Katie nodded but still didn't look higher than his chest. What a lousy way to end a perfect evening. He was probably glad he wouldn't see her tomorrow after this.

"I'll miss you tomorrow." The whispered words in her ear stirred up a whole hurricane of flutters in her belly.

"You will?" She had to know if he was telling the truth and glanced up. His eyes met hers, and a flame of longing shot between them.

"I will. And every day until I get to see you again." He crooked his finger under her chin. "And I do plan to see you again."

"Even after …" She waved her hand back toward the stadium.

"This was the best night of my life." He pressed a kiss to her lips before she could protest. She raised to her tiptoes so she could reach him better, winding her hands around his waist. It was the best night for her too. Ever.

When he opened the door for her to climb in, both of them were slightly breathless. How long before they could get together again? Had he said? She didn't even notice the traffic around them. Nothing mattered but living until the next time she could see her Beast.

# 13

"Katie." Someone nudged her shoulder. "Katie, wake up. We've got a problem."

What time was it? There was no way she'd been in bed long enough for it to be time to rise again. She swatted at the relentless hand that poked her.

"Katie, seriously. Your friend is gone." Jodie's words penetrated Katie's sleep-deprived brain.

"What?" Katie rolled over and met eyes with Bree, who was blinking beside her. "She's right here."

"Your other friend." Jodie smacked Katie's arm. "Skye. She's gone."

"Gone?" Katie sat up and felt Bree doing the same. "How could she be gone?"

"Nick heard the alarm going off early this morning and got up to check all the doors. Evidently Skye decided to leave at daybreak and had walked out the front door. But by the time Nick figured out what had happened, she'd already gotten into a little red sedan and was heading down the road."

"Ryan." Bree's voice anchored Katie's thoughts for a second.

Skye had run off with Ryan? At dawn? Why?

"I don't understand. Why would she do this?" Katie rubbed her forehead. "She never gets up early."

"Do you have any messages on your phone?" Jodie pointed to the device plugged in on the bedside table.

"None over here." Bree slid her finger over her screen.

"No. Nothing." Katie ran a hand through her hair. They'd gotten in around midnight, just like Jodie had predicted. Skye couldn't have gotten a full six hours of sleep.

"I'm going to call her." Bree stood and paced back and forth, her cell pressed to her ear. "She's not picking up. Maybe she'll answer a text."

"Don't you have her on that app that lets you keep track of where your friends are? You used it the other night with me. Maybe we can do the same with her?"

Katie strained her brain to figure out what could have prompted Skye to leave without at least letting them know where she was going. Sure, she was a grown woman, but she'd supposedly come on this trip to spend time with her girl-friends. From where Katie sat, that was hard to do when she'd run off with a guy.

"Maybe she turned off her phone or something." Bree tossed her phone on the bed. "She didn't show up on my map."

"So much for one last day together." Katie pulled her knees to her chest and rested her chin on them.

"She's acted flightier than normal this trip, I admit." Bree sat beside Katie and leaned her head on her shoulder. "But this is extreme even for her. Picking up boys is one thing. Running off with them is something totally different."

"Aunt Katie!" Riley rushed into the room and jumped onto the mattress.

"Hey, Riley-bug. What's up?" She crossed her legs and pulled him into her lap.

"Can you play dinosaurs with me this morning? I'll let you be the T-Rex." He pressed his little hands onto each of her cheeks and squeezed a bit.

"Sorry, bud. I have to figure out where Ms. Skye went first, okay? But I promise to play with you before we leave tomorrow."

"Skye went to the coasters." Riley shrugged. "She said they were more fun than a mountain."

"What did you say?" All three girls leaned closer to him.

"I heard her talking to that guy yesterday. She kept talking about coasters. What's a coaster?" Riley looked over his shoulder at Jodie.

"It's a big ride that goes way up high and then around and around." Jodie motioned with her hands to act like one of the cars. "At least, I think that's what it is. Assuming I'm understanding what you're saying correctly."

"You probably are." Bree pursed her lips for a second. "Skye pointed out a Six Flags billboard yesterday, talking about how she hadn't been in forever. I bet that's where they went. Remember how she wasn't thrilled with the idea of going to Stone Mountain?"

"She hasn't liked any of my ideas for this trip." A strand of hair fell over her forehead, and Katie huffed out a breath to move it. "But we've pretty much done exactly what she wanted up to this point. Why should she do anything else now?"

"Hey." Bree squeezed Katie's shoulder. "We'll find her and figure this out. Maybe Camden can call Ryan?"

Camden. Could he have known about this? Her heart clenched in her chest. No. He'd said his uncle wanted Ryan to stay home. Besides, he would've warned her.

It wasn't even seven o'clock. He'd probably gotten in just as late as they had. Would he be awake?

"Just call him and ask. If his cousin has run off with Skye, he'll probably want to know." Bree's logic didn't settle Katie's churning emotions.

She slid her fingers down the screen and pushed his contact. The phone emblem lit up, showing that the call was going through. She held it to her ear just in time to hear a sleepy, "Katie?"

"Hey, Camden. Do you know where Ryan is?"

Rustling sounds came from the other end of the line. "Ryan?"

"Yeah. Your cousin. We think Skye is with him." Katie was having trouble keeping the sarcasm out of her voice.

"Hang on." Camden sounded more awake by the moment but didn't sound happy.

Katie listened to various grunts and breathing through the phone. What was he doing? He groaned and a door slammed in her ear.

"He's not here. Hang on. Let me check and see if I have any messages." More shuffling noises. "No. Nothing. Uncle John may kill him."

Katie let her head fall back against the headboard with a thump. "Great."

"Do you know when Skye left?" Camden's voice was full of frustration, and Katie imagined him dashing his fingers through his hair like he did when upset. Had she really gotten to know him so well in such a short time?

"No. Not exactly. Nick heard the alarm go off around dawn and went to check. He saw a red car pulling away down the road. And Skye was gone. Riley thinks they were going to ride roller coasters."

"Roller coasters?"

"Yeah. Riley said Skye said coasters were more fun than mountains. And yesterday Skye got all excited when we saw a billboard for Six Flags." Katie winked at the boy who came to her door at the sound of his name. He shut and opened both eyes in return, then ran off, a stegosaurus in one hand and a pterodactyl in the other.

"But the park doesn't open until after ten, if I remember correctly. Why would they leave so early?"

"It does take a while to get around in this city. Maybe they were trying to beat the bad traffic?" Katie glanced at Bree who was frowning.

"Even with bad traffic, it wouldn't take them three or more hours to get across the city. Maybe an hour or so from Jodie's house." Camden huffed. "Let me see if I can call Ryan. I guess you already tried calling her?"

"We think her phone is off." Katie tapped her fingers against her knees. "No answers to calls or texts, and we can't find her on the app Bree uses to stalk us."

"I don't stalk you." Bree gave her a light pinch.

"Okay. I'll see what I can find out and call you back in a bit." Camden paused. "Katie? It's going to be okay."

"Sure." She swallowed a lump in her throat. "Thanks."

Camden jerked the pillow off his bed, threw it back down, and pummeled it ten or eleven times. Considering he was under Uncle John's roof, he shouldn't have to be responsible for his cousin's bad choices. But because Ryan had run off with Katie's friend, and he knew Katie would be distraught about it, now it was his problem too.

He picked up his cell phone and dialed Ryan. As expected, no answer. He shot off an angry text and threw his phone back down, cringing as it hit the desk harder than intended. Time to get dressed and face the wrath of Ryan's dad.

Of all the foolish things Ryan could've done. Camden had planned to sleep in, pack his things, and head home today. So much for that. Now, not only had Ryan ruined Camden's plans, he'd ruined Katie's too. And considering how well she handled having craziness thrust on her, she was probably freaking out right now.

Would this mess things up with him and her? It better not. Because even though Ryan might not be ready to settle down or grow up, Camden was beyond ready to have someone like Katie in his life for all time.

"What's wrong?" Uncle John looked up from his morning paper as Camden stormed into the breakfast nook.

"Ryan's gone." No need to mince words. His uncle was a businessman through and through. He'd want it as straightforward as possible.

"Gone?" Uncle John set down his coffee.

"We think he picked up Skye with plans to head to Six Flags for the day, but we're not sure. Evidently she snuck out around sunrise with no note or explanation." Camden poured a cup of coffee and leaned against the kitchen counter.

Uncle John folded the paper neatly, pressing the creases straight. A short eternity later, the older man leaned back and directed his attention to Camden again. Nothing but calmness showed in every movement—exacerbating Camden's own erratic frustration.

"Why do you expect them to be heading to Six Flags?" Uncle John crossed his arms over his chest. "They don't open until later, right? No need to leave so early for that. And why would they sneak around if they were going there?"

"We haven't figured out any of that. Unless they just left early to get away without having to answer any questions.

Neither one of them is answering their phone or text messages." Camden dashed a hand through his hair, wincing as several strands came loose with the fury of his action.

"This is one of those girls you two hung out with all week? The ones you took to the ballgame last night?" Uncle John raised an eyebrow as if to say, *See what happens when you run around with trash?*

"Yes. But Bree and Katie don't know any more than I do. The only reason we think Six Flags is because Katie's nephew overheard Skye say something about coasters being fun." Camden set his mug down in the sink, empty. He didn't even remember drinking the stuff, and it sure wasn't helping clear his head like he'd hoped.

Uncle John picked up his own phone and tapped a few times. "Looks like they're on the east side of the city, maybe stopped at a diner or something."

"You can track him?" Camden pushed away from the counter.

"I made sure when he got this phone that it allowed me to know where it was at all times. I feel that's only fair since I'm the one paying for everything." Uncle John set his phone aside again and took one more sip of coffee. "Are you still thinking you'll leave today?"

That was it? He wasn't going to worry about this? He wasn't upset?

"I don't know. I imagine Katie and Bree are going to be rather upset about their friend ditching them. I thought I might go check on them, see if there's anything I can do. Depending on how long that takes, I might head back anyway. I'm rather tired of trying to be his chaperone."

"I never expected you to be a chaperone for him." Uncle John turned from the sink. "I just wanted you with him to be a good influence. It may not seem like it now, but you have been."

Really? "I don't feel like I had much influence at all."

"You'd be surprised." His uncle nodded, tucking the paper under his arm. "But I also wanted you to go on the trip with him because I knew you needed a break. You've been working hard these last few years. You deserved to have some fun too. I hope you were able to enjoy yourself at least a little bit this week."

Camden might as well have been handed a medal from the president himself. He couldn't have been more shocked, that was sure. When his mom had first mentioned Uncle John's intentions to include him on Ryan's trip, she'd insinuated he was basically to be a babysitter and make sure his cousin didn't do anything stupid. Had they both been wrong?

And yet the weight of responsibility remained on his shoulders despite what his uncle had just said. Should he look at the situation as unworried as Ryan's father? Did Katie actually need him to do anything, or should he just go home as planned?

"By the way." Uncle John leaned back into the kitchen again. "I'll keep an eye on Ryan and let you know if their plans change. But I imagine what your friends have deduced is probably true. And Six Flags is fairly harmless. If they were headed to Las Vegas or something, that would be another story."

The smirk Uncle John shot him before he wandered down the hall again brought a small grin to Camden's own lips. His uncle was right. Katie's panic had rubbed off on him this morning, and he'd jumped to conclusions much worse than reality.

*God, please keep Ryan and Skye safe today. Help them to enjoy whatever they have planned. And help Katie and Bree to have a great day too.* Camden shot up the quick prayer and then headed to gather his few things. No matter what, he'd go on home today. He wasn't really in the mood to face his cousin again anyway.

"Camden?" Katie answered her phone before it had even had a chance for a full ring.

"Hey, Katie. Uncle John checked his phone's tracking app and said Ryan's somewhere on the east side of town. Looked like maybe a diner. We're betting they're probably eating breakfast and biding time until the park opens." Camden sniffed a pair of socks and wrinkled his nose before throwing them in his duffle. He'd just wash everything when he got home instead of worrying about how clean things might be now.

"Did he call him? Did Ryan explain why?" Katie's voice still held an edge of panic and chaos.

"No. Ryan didn't answer. But Uncle John's going to keep an eye on the app throughout the day and make sure nothing changes from what we've figured out." Camden got on his knees and ran a hand under the bed to make sure he hadn't missed anything. "He didn't seem worried at all."

"So, that's it?"

"That's what?" Camden wiggled the bag's zipper until it followed the path around the flap like it was supposed to.

"Skye ruined our day, and we're not supposed to worry about it because your uncle isn't?" He could almost see her pacing in his mind. She was working herself into the size of tizzy he'd seen when they first met. Going back to that memory just made him want to see her again before he headed for Tennessee. Not that she'd loved being held at that time, but she'd still felt good in his arms.

"Katie, this doesn't have to ruin your day. Calm down." Camden lowered himself to the edge of the bed.

"Calm down?" She huffed into his ear. "That's great advice,

Camden. Sure. I have no idea if my friend is safe or not, but I'll calm down. No worries."

"Hey." He leaned forward and rested his elbows on his knees. "Ryan isn't going to hurt her. She'll be fine."

"And how do you know this when you didn't get them to answer the phone either? I'll just bet—"

"Camden? Hey, it's Bree." Bree's voice broke through whatever Katie had been about to say. "Sorry about this. I'll try and calm her down. Thanks for following up for us."

"Is she going to be okay, Bree? I was about to head for home, but I don't want to worry about her all day." Camden fiddled with the strap of his bag.

"I'll talk her down."

Despite Katie's voice being muffled in the background, he could tell from the tone she was giving Bree an earful. Scuffling sounds came through the line, then nothing. He pulled the device away from his ear and looked. The call had been ended ... by accident or on purpose, he had no idea.

He waited a few minutes to see if she'd call back, but the phone remained silent. Right. Like he'd be a safe driver if he left now. Looked like he needed to drive in the opposite direction before heading back to Tennessee. Time to see if he could help Bree talk Katie down.

# 14

Thirty minutes later, Camden shifted his weight back and forth between feet as he stood on Jodie's porch. The curtain shifted for a second, and then Bree opened the door. A frown wrinkled her forehead, and she let out a sigh.

"I was afraid you'd come."

Not the greeting he'd hoped for. "I'm sorry?"

"I'm just not sure if it's going to help or not. Katie is ... well, come on in and you'll see." Bree stepped back, allowing him into the house.

It was quieter than he expected. From the way Katie had ranted at him earlier, he'd braced himself for more of that. Instead, quiet sounds of Riley driving his cars down the hallway and the tick of a clock on the mantel were all he heard. It was as if the house held its breath, waiting for an explosion to occur any second. He followed Bree into the kitchen.

"Hey, Camden." Jodie looked back from where she'd been staring out the door to the back porch.

He was about to ask where Katie was when he saw the movement through the glass. She paced the deck like a

143

panther, stalking back and forth, her hands slicing through the air as she muttered to herself. Even on the other side of the wall, he could sense the anger radiating off her in waves. Had something else happened? This seemed a bit extreme for having a friend ditch her for the day.

"I sent her out there until she could calm down." Jodie waved her hand toward the outside. "She was upsetting Riley. And I couldn't handle the yelling and shrieking anymore."

"Is she this upset because of Skye and Ryan, or is there something else?" Camden leaned against the doorframe and watched her, his heart picking up every time she passed the window. How could he help her? He'd never seen anyone this angry before.

"Skye and Ryan triggered it, but I think it's been building for a while." Bree picked up a mug of coffee and stuck it in the microwave. "At least all week."

"Probably more like ten years." Jodie lightly beat her fist against the armrest of her wheelchair.

"Ten years?" Camden tore his eyes off the younger sister to focus on the older.

Jodie didn't elaborate.

"Aren't you glad you came?" Bree took a sip of her reheated drink. "I've never seen her this worked up. Both of us have tried, but all she does is put up more hackles, more walls. It's like she doesn't want to calm down and think rationally anymore."

"I mean, I'm willing to try, if you think it would help. But you both know more about her history than I do. I definitely don't know ten years' worth." Camden crossed his arms.

"You two seemed to have hit it off really well. Looked like you had several things in common and a mutual understanding." Jodie turned toward him. "But if you really are interested in my sister, it's better you see this side of her now. Because she needs help. She won't admit it, but she does. Seeing her like this, though, can either strengthen the relationship you two have been growing this week ... or it can kill it before it has a real chance."

He clenched and unclenched his fists. Killing the chance of a relationship with Katie wasn't what he wanted. But he wasn't a psychologist or anything. How was he supposed to help her through this when he didn't even know the full story? His eyes darted to the window as Katie froze. She was looking directly at him, and his pulse skipped a beat. Now he knew what an antelope felt like when a lioness caught it in her sights.

"Too late now." He moved toward the door. "She knows I'm here."

"Good luck." Bree squeezed his arm as he walked by.

He stepped through the door and pulled it closed behind him. She didn't move. Didn't acknowledge him. Nothing.

"I wanted to make sure you were okay." That was a good start, right? Peaceable. Kind. Thoughtful? Unselfish?

"Do I *look* okay?" Her words were clipped, tone deep and sarcastic.

Should he try the truth? She always looked great to him, but that wasn't what she meant. He refused to back away, though. He took a tentative step her direction.

"I've never seen your hair in a ponytail before." Maybe a change of subject would be easier. Not that they'd really broached a subject yet. "It's cute."

Her jaw worked like she was holding back several choice phrases. "What do you want, Camden? You obviously don't care about me any more than anyone else."

Really? He'd driven all the way over here, out of his way, because he didn't care? What could he say to someone being completely irrational? Would anything reach her?

"You can believe that if you want to. Doesn't make it true." He moved slowly to her left and propped one hip on the edge of the picnic table. "Your sister's yard is nice."

A ramp ambled down off the porch to a concrete path that wound through the landscaped lawn. A swing set took up one corner, a vegetable garden another. The porch had fans above them to move the sticky Georgia air around and keep things semi-pleasant. He wouldn't mind a yard like this of his own one day. Would Katie want something like this, even including the playscape for future children? One glance at her showed she wasn't in a mood for talking about any possibilities that might lead to such a scenario.

"You drove all this way to see my sister's back yard?" She had her hands on her hips, and it took everything in him not to scoop her up and kiss her until she started thinking reasonably again.

"I came all this way because it worried me the way our phone call ended earlier." He scooted farther onto the table and propped his elbows on his knees. "Because I thought we had a good thing going last night, but the way you hung up on me this morning left me wondering if I'd ever hear from you again. Not to mention, I thought maybe there'd be a stronger possibility of you believing me if you could see my face."

"And what am I supposed to believe?" She shifted her weight from one leg to the other. "Besides that you supposedly care about me."

"Well, for one thing, I wanted to make sure you understood I had nothing to do with Ryan and Skye sneaking off this morning. I was as flabbergasted as you."

"*Flabbergasted.*" She snorted. "That's one word for it, I guess."

"Secondly, I wanted to confirm I was just as concerned about them as you until we had all the pieces together and figured out where they were headed. And, by the way, Uncle John texted me right as I got here. They are indeed at Six Flags."

There went her jaw again, working back and forth. Her eyes shimmered as she turned toward the yard and away from him.

"So, why aren't you and Bree doing Stone Mountain like you'd originally planned? Did Skye not leave her car keys for y'all?"

She spun around. "We can't just take her car! She's not here."

"You've been driving it all week." He frowned. "Why should today be any different?"

"Because she's not here. She, in her selfishness, decided once again that we didn't need to do what I wanted to do. That only her wishes mattered. So, she snuck out and scared us half to death. And left it so we can't do anything either."

"So, see if Jodie will let you borrow a car. Or call a ride share. Or something." He tucked his hands under his legs to keep from reaching out and shaking her. "You're only letting Skye win if you stay here angry and hurt all day."

"I don't have an uncle or a daddy paying for my trip like you, Camden. I'm paying for this trip with the measly little funds I was able to scrape together working at the school library the last few years. I can't just call a cab and drive to a state park. And what if there wasn't someone available to bring us back? No. Skye won once again. But after Bree's wedding, I won't have to see her again. She can go off and waste her life however she wants, and I can settle into mine."

"Skye is only winning because you're letting her." He stood and dug out his wallet. He pulled out the hundred-dollar bill his uncle had given him to help cover gas and groceries. "Here. If you need money for a ride, this should be enough."

"I'm not taking your money." She pushed it away. "Is that

supposed to make up for letting Ryan out of your sight this morning? I mean, wasn't it your job to be a good influence on him and keep him out of trouble?"

He swallowed the anger that bubbled up inside him at those remarks. No need to stoop to her level. "Ryan can make his own bad choices. In fact, Uncle John informed me this morning that he hadn't intended for me to be a babysitter. He just figured I deserved a vacation, too, since I hadn't had one in a few years. And he hoped by my tagging along that Ryan would make better choices. I thought he had until today."

"What are you saying?" She narrowed her eyes.

"I'm saying that when he decided to tag along with you all, I was glad. I didn't know if it would end well, but you intrigued me. I loved your fiery temper, your curls that go everywhere, your passion about history and books. I even wanted to know more about what made you tick, what made you so worried Monday night, everything."

Had her stance softened just a bit?

"And I was glad I'd have the chance. But maybe I was wrong. Maybe all that other stuff just covered up this selfish little girl who is ruining Bree's last day of vacation because she didn't get her way."

"Selfish!" She stomped her foot. "Skye's the one who is self-ish. She's the one ruining everything."

"Really?" He lightly poked her shoulder. "Because from where I stand, you're the one keeping you and Bree from having a good time today. You know you could take Skye's car and stick to your plans, but you chose to throw a fit instead. You've upset your sister, your nephew, and your best friend. And I drove over half an hour in the wrong direction to check on you before I headed home. Guess I wasted my time." He made it all the way back across the porch and had his hand on the door handle.

Finally, she quit spluttering. "I guess you wasted your whole week. Obviously, I am too much for you."

"Yeah." He didn't even turn around to look at her for fear he'd give in and go back over there to try his first urge—kissing her senseless. "I guess you are."

---

Was Katie really just going to stand here and let him walk away? Half of her yearned to reach out and ask him to wait, to throw herself into his arms, to stop him before he walked out of her life for good. But the stubborn, mulish side of her was stronger, holding on to the temper that had been slowly ebbing over the last few minutes.

Hadn't he added at least an hour to his trip home simply to check on her? And she'd basically told him that everything they'd been building and growing this week was nothing more than a weed to be thrown into the fire. She plopped down on the seat of the picnic table and wrapped her arms around herself as the tears slowly leaked from her eyes.

He'd stayed with her through her panic attacks, her rants about the guys following them to the beach, and even her standoffishness that first day in Louisiana. And she ruined everything. For what?

"Katie?" Bree's voice was tentative.

Jodie followed her friend out onto the porch. "You okay?"

"No." Katie studied her hands clasped in her lap. "I may never be okay again."

"That's a bit dramatic, even for you." Jodie squeezed her shoulder. "Why did he leave you this money?"

Katie cringed at the folded-up bill in Jodie's hand. "I told him we couldn't go to Stone Mountain because it wasn't right to take Skye's car without her permission and I couldn't afford to call a cab. He probably needs that more than I did. His uncle paid for his trip, and he said something about heading home, so I'm sure he'll need gas money."

"Well, he handed it to me and told me to chase you out to do what you wanted in the first place and not let Skye hold you back." Jodie pressed it into her hands.

"I guess I'll have to find a way to get it back to him." Katie flipped it over and over. "Maybe I can get a mailing address from Ryan through Skye."

"You're going to talk to Skye after this?" Bree raised her eyebrows.

"I don't really have a choice. I mean, she's our ride to Germantown tomorrow. I'm just glad she's heading home to St. Louis the next day." Katie closed her eyes.

"We could still go." Bree hooked a thumb toward the driveway. "I don't have any qualms about taking her car. If she didn't want us to use it, she should've taken it herself."

"Bree!"

"What?" Bree grinned. "I'd love to go see Stone Mountain with you. And without Skye, we can just hike to the top and not worry about making sure she gets on the tram first. You know she didn't want to do the climb."

"You guys should stay for the laser show too." Jodie nodded. "Go pack a picnic dinner to take. You can eat lunch and then head out. That gives you plenty of time. I have an old blanket you can take to sit on for the show."

"I wish you'd come with us. Riley would love it." Katie stood and dusted her britches.

"Can you imagine me rolling this thing up the side of a mountain? No thank you." Jodie maneuvered her chair back into the house. "And don't get me started on the energy it takes to keep a three-year-old from getting hurt on a huge chunk of granite like that."

"You could ride to the top." Bree shrugged. "It's what Skye was going to do."

"Have you seen that thing?" Jodie shuddered. "It hangs there, in midair, with nothing underneath it. No. This girl doesn't do heights if she can at all avoid it."

"I should be the one in the wheelchair." Katie pushed the door closed with more force than necessary. "It's not fair that it's you instead of me."

"Sounds like we need to finally talk more about that when you get back tonight, huh?" Jodie gave her a no-nonsense look that was scarily like their mom's.

"I don't know what you're talking about." Katie dug out sandwich supplies from the fridge.

"You'll find out."

"There's incentive to come back early." Katie slammed the mustard on the counter.

"Katherine Denise Wilhite, you've been obsessing over this wreck for ten years. There is literally nothing you could have done differently. You were twelve years old. Let it go."

"How can I let it go? It ruined your life. And mine. Did you know I've had two panic attacks this week? Two! Because of that night, I can't go anywhere." Katie dashed away tears threatening to leak down her cheeks.

"Katie. You weren't even a teenager yet. You weren't driving. You weren't anywhere around the guy who hit us, so there was nothing you could do there. The whole situation was out of your control."

"I could've sat on the side of the car I normally sat on. But I threw that big fit, remember? I can't even recall why, but I wanted to swap sides with you, and Mom finally made you agree just to get me to quit fussing. And the side I normally sat on, where you were, was the side that got hit. It should have been me with the broken back. Not you." Katie turned her back on her sister, unwilling to let her see the anguish surely written on her face.

"Katie." Jodie rubbed her arm. "It's my fault. I lied to you and told you the Christmas lights were better on that side of the car to make you want to sit there. I wanted to be where I was because I had more leg room behind mom. Besides, my life isn't ruined. I can still drive myself around, and I have Nick and Riley, and I work from a computer, so I'd have to sit down for that anyway. Besides, what would my arms look like if I didn't have to use them so much? I'd never have these amazing muscles if I hadn't been in that wreck."

Katie turned and wiped away more moisture. "You're crazy."

"That's why you love me so much." Jodie winked. "So, get packed. We'll have a quick lunch, and you can go explore a mountain this afternoon. Think about other things."

"Is it lunch time, Mama?" Riley dashed through the door and leapt onto Jodie's lap. "I want peanut butter. Okay?"

"Okay, baby. Let's let Aunt Katie pack her picnic first, though, okay?"

"Are we going on a picnic?" The three-year-old squirmed out of his mother's arms. "Yippee! I've gotta go pack my dinosaurs."

"Freeze, squirt!" Katie caught him around the middle before he could run out again. "Today, it's just going to be Ms. Bree and Aunt Katie on the picnic, okay? But your mama says you get to come see me later this summer, and we'll have one together then, okay?"

His little brow furrowed as he considered the proposition. "I guess. But why can't I do both?"

"Because Aunt Katie is going to climb a big, tall mountain, and it might be dangerous." Katie widened her eyes. "I'll come back and take you to climb it when you're older, okay?"

"Promise?"

"Promise." She pressed her forehead to his for a moment and then released him.

Katie threw together two ham sandwiches for their evening meal and then helped her sister prepare lunch. "Where did Bree get to?"

"I think she left when you and I started talking about the wreck." Jodie cut Riley's sandwich in half and then added a handful of grapes to his plate.

"I found them!" Bree dangled Skye's car keys in her right hand. "Figured I better make sure we really could get there now that we've talked you into it."

Jodie and Bree and Riley all chatted happily through lunch, but Katie only contributed to the conversation when necessary. Her mind was on the tall, blond man with the blue eyes who'd stormed out of here earlier. The one she'd chased away. How was she ever going to make this better? Could she? Was there any way to make things right after she'd broken them so thoroughly?

# 15

"Why did we think this was a good idea again?" Katie huffed out a shallow breath as she paused on the side of the mountain. "I mean, who looks at these big chunks of rock and thinks, 'Ooh! I bet I could climb that.'"

"Just think of the view we'll have from the top. We're over halfway now." Bree gave her a little push from behind.

"The problem with being over halfway is the top is steeper than the bottom. This is the hard part." Katie studied the granite ahead of her.

It wasn't straight up, but it wasn't gradual either. A family with small children passed her and Bree. Okay. If people with toddlers could handle this monstrosity, so could she. It wasn't the scariest mountain she'd faced this day. Of course, her track record wasn't that great either.

What would Camden think of her mentally calling him a mountain? He'd probably raise one of those perfect eyebrows, and one corner of his mouth would go up in that adorable smirk. He'd cross his arms, highlighting the toned muscles there. And she needed to quit thinking about him before her heartrate accelerated too much higher. Besides, she'd ruined that chance.

Probably just as well, but painful, nonetheless.

"Katie?" Bree reached out and used a branch of a bush to help herself get a little higher.

"Hm?" Katie pulled her thoughts away from the man she'd driven away in anger that morning.

"Was Skye right?"

Well, that wasn't what Katie had expected to hear. "About what?"

"About you being upset about my getting married?" Bree paused and looked down at her.

Katie stopped and rested her hands on her knees, making it look like she was catching her breath. "Why would I be upset about that? You know I think you're great together."

Bree shook her head. "Don't think I don't know what you're doing. You always answer a question with a question when you're avoiding it. I guess that means you are upset."

"Bree!" Katie couldn't race after her friend. Not on a grade this steep. But she could hoof it after her as fast as gravity would allow.

At the top, the mound of granite rounded off, and a blessedly air-conditioned building sat several feet away. It was where the tram came up on the other side of the mountain for those who weren't stupid enough to climb the thing. Bree bypassed the structure and walked down to the fence, where various other park guests milled around, staring out at the scenery.

Below them was the sculptured side of the mountain, where the laser show performed each evening. Katie took in the view, catching her breath and trying to understand how she and Bree had somehow gotten on the wrong foot now too.

It was bad enough she'd ostracized two others today—well, Skye did it to herself—but Camden ...

"Bree, I'm thrilled for you." Katie ran a finger over the top of the fence.

"But?"

"But everything is changing all at once. I've had you as my best friend for almost four years now. I had my safe place at school. I knew exactly what to expect from everything. And now that we've graduated, I'm moving to a whole new area. I have a job I've never officially done before, and you're going off in a few weeks to start your life with Nathan ... four hours away. I'm going to miss you."

"But you have me for the next month. Remember? I'm still rooming with you until the wedding." Bree bumped shoulders with her.

"I know. But then you won't." Katie glanced at her from the corner of her eye. "Sort of feels like I'm being left behind."

"Not left behind. Just left going in a different direction." Bree side hugged her. "Besides, you'll be sick of me by then because you know all I ever do is talk about wedding plans and Nathan. And you've got Camden now."

"No."

"No?" Bree leaned away. "Girl, he came out of his way just to check on you this morning. That boy is smitten."

"I told him he made a mistake coming. Made a mistake with the whole week." Katie turned slightly and stared, unseeing, in the other direction. "Is that part of the Olympic stadium?"

"Don't change the subject." Bree tugged on her arm. "But yes, it is."

"Bree, I know you want me to have the happiness you and Nathan have. And you make it look wonderful, trust me. But I think

I'm just too broken to handle a relationship. Who wants someone who can't even walk down a street without having a panic attack? Or can't handle a slight change in plans without going all to pieces? I wouldn't even want to deal with someone like that."

"Katie, I don't know if you noticed or not, but your panic attacks didn't scare him away. If anything, they made him hover over you more." Bree tilted her head. "Maybe he's been looking for a damsel in distress so he can play the hero."

It was so close to the flirty banter she and Camden had tossed back and forth between each other all week she had to swallow a little sob. She'd labeled him the beast the other night, but it wasn't true. If anyone had been a beast in their relationship this week, it was her.

"You've got his number. Why don't you apologize?" Bree turned and started back towards the building. "I'm going to see if they have a water fountain or something in here before I start the trek back down."

"Bree, I can't." Katie tightened her ponytail. "I can't. It's better this way. Just leave it as a fun little vacation romance. No expectations. No worries. We won't even have to figure out how to see each other. I mean, I know he lives in Tennessee, but that's not exactly a short state. What if he lives closer to your end of the state than mine? I'm just getting settled in Germantown, and it would look awful if I didn't work even a full year at this job. I mean, they could've hired just about anyone, but they chose me."

"You're borrowing trouble." Bree grabbed Katie's hand and tugged. "No more worrying about it now. I've got several weeks to wear you down before I become Mrs. Nathan Miller. I'm not giving up whether you say you are or not."

"Why did I think it was a good idea to have you as my roommate until the wedding?" Katie followed her towards the bathrooms.

"Because it helps with the rent until your paycheck starts coming in." Bree winked. "And because you're going to miss me."

The hike back down took almost as much care and exertion as going up. Due to the steep grade near the top, they had to place their feet carefully and make sure the soles of their shoes didn't slip. At least three times, Katie or Bree reached out and grabbed the other to slow down a mite. It was a huge relief to reach the bottom.

Katie looked back up, awed at the giant she'd climbed. It wasn't a huge mountain compared to many others in the world. But it was the largest she'd ever conquered. Maybe it was a sign of good things to come. But she couldn't handle two in one day. This one was enough for now.

They lazed the remainder of the afternoon, hiking a short trail, picnicking, admiring a few of the monuments, and finding a good spot for the laser show that started at dusk. As they lounged on the blanket Jodie had sent with them, Katie tried to focus on the stars popping out in the blackening sky, the murmurs of hundreds of conversations around them, the happy chatter of her best friend beside her.

Instead, her mind wandered off. Which direction had Camden driven this morning? Was he home yet? Was he upset about how things ended, too, or glad to be rid of her?

"Do you think Skye had a fun day?" Bree's question broke into Katie's depressing thoughts.

"I honestly don't care one way or the other, but I imagine she has. She's one of those people who makes fun wherever they go." Katie tucked her knees to her and rested her chin on them. "I'm sort of dreading facing her tonight."

"Yeah. She probably has no idea how much she upset us this morning." Bree twirled a blade of grass in her fingers.

"Do you think she cares?" Katie huffed.

"She is our friend, whether you feel friendly toward her right now or not." Bree nudged Katie's arm. "And we were mostly upset because we were worried about her, right?"

"And upset because, once again, she tried to make sure that only her plans got put into action instead of mine." Katie knew her voice sounded a little whiny, but she couldn't help it. "She's just selfish, Bree. She didn't think of anyone else when she left this morning."

"And yet she offered the use of her car for this trip and paid for most of the hotel in New Orleans. And talked her aunt into letting us stay in the condo too." Bree leaned forward to meet Katie's eyes. "That isn't selfish."

Katie shook her head. She had no reply, but she also couldn't completely agree with Bree that Skye wasn't selfish. Everything Skye had done this trip had been for her own pleasure, caring nothing about what Katie wanted.

"It's all Skye's fault that we've had so much craziness this week. If she hadn't invited the boys to go along with us that first night, none of this would have happened. I could've asked Camden to leave me alone, and that would have been it. Just a bump on the head and a dunk in the pool. No other injuries."

"Like a broken heart?" Bree squeezed Katie from the side.

"Look. The show's about to start."

"Katie, you're letting the bad overshadow the good." Bree leaned close to be heard over the music. "If you'd stop to think, this week hasn't been what we planned or expected, but it hasn't been bad either."

Katie kept her eyes fixed on the side of the mountain, unwilling to look at her best friend. The tears threatening to escape might drip down and be noticeable. Better to pretend to watch the patriotic scenes playing out in lasers and lights on the granite backdrop.

But Bree was right, as always. Camden had surprised her in

a good way time and again. The carriage ride, the concern over the fire ant bites, the ride on the ferry, the dinner at the fancy Cajun restaurant, the walks along the beach, the fajitas and s'mores at the condo, the kisses, the Braves game. Coming over to make sure she was okay this morning shouldn't have surprised her at all. Because that's the kind of guy he is.

Much as she was glad to finally have time with just Bree this week, she missed him like crazy as she sat in the thick, warm Atlanta night. He'd encouraged her to come, not to give up her whole day simply because her friend had ditched her for something else. He'd suggested the light show. But he wasn't here to share it.

And now she'd probably never see him again to thank him.

***

A strange number glowed on Camden's phone screen as he walked through his kitchen that evening. He frowned and swiped the screen to read the message.

Camden, it's Bree. I stole your number from Katie. Hope you don't mind too much. I just wanted to let you know she's regretting her words from this morning. We've talked some this afternoon, and you're her main topic. I hope you won't give up.

Camden released a long sigh. Give up? Give up on what? Was there anything left to hold on to? Katie had informed him that morning that the whole week had been a mistake.

Every time he closed his eyes, her curl-framed face with her fiery hazel eyes filled his mind. He'd seen just about every side of her now. Mad. Panicking. Tired. Happy. In love?

He shook his head and cleared it of her image. The apology would've meant more if it had come from Katie instead of her best friend. It was all well and good that Katie had been talking about him to Bree, and it did intrigue him. But could he forgive her without a direct request for forgiveness? His conscience twinged. He knew he was supposed to forgive no matter what.

But it would be easier if he wasn't taking someone else's word for it that Katie was sorry. He tapped the edge of his phone against his leg. It was Friday. The girls should get home tomorrow. Did he dare try the plan he'd come up with last night?

She hadn't completely driven him away this morning. Sure, he'd hated the words coming out of her mouth, but he also knew there was more to it. All week long, she'd joked about not being able to handle changes. He sat on one of his bar stools and leaned on the counter. But why couldn't she? Why did it upset her so much when things happened out of her control?

Thanks for letting me know, Bree. And of course it's okay for you to have my number.

He sent the message back before he could stop himself. Staying in contact with her friends was the best he could get right now, so he'd take it.

I'm rooming with her for the next few weeks, so I'll keep working on her.

Bree ended her reply with a winky emoji.

He chuckled at the image that produced. Bree did have some tenacity that just might change her friend's mind. And having her around Katie for a while longer might help with his other idea too. Was he completely nuts to want to try this? Who kept pursuing a girl who told him to quit?

"If I'm nuts, then I'm going to be nuts all the way." He muttered to himself and hopped down to pace again.

Would this work? It couldn't hurt, right? After all, it would be the neighborly thing to do. And she'd need somewhere to worship when she got settled, no matter what.

Was he seriously pacing the short length of his galley kitchen, justifying his actions to himself? Maybe he was crazier than he thought. But he'd do it anyway.

Before he could change his mind, he shot off one more text to Bree.

I have an idea.

Words that had gotten them in trouble before. Words that might cause more turmoil now. But they were gone into the cloud. No way to fetch them back.

I'm in.

Bree's response came almost immediately.

Just tell me what to do, and I'll help.

He hadn't even told her what he was thinking yet. If he could get Bree to trust him so implicitly, maybe he had more of a chance with her friend than he thought. He sure hoped so.

As his phone's screen saver kicked on, Katie's smile from the baseball game filled the area where the message boxes had been. Somehow, someway, he had to see her again. And his ideas had to be better than Ryan's ideas had been this week, right?

# 16

"You went home?" Ryan's voice screamed skepticism through Camden's phone when he answered that evening.

"Yes. I told you I probably would." Camden shook his head. "I mean it's not like our trip wasn't over. The girls were supposed to be climbing a mountain, and I wanted to let them have at least one day together without us since it's their last trip before Bree's wedding. If you hadn't messed that up, they probably would've had a great time."

Ryan's snort came through the connection loud and clear. "Oh, please. There's no way Skye would've had a good time climbing a mountain. Wait. Did you say I messed it up?"

"Yes. I was rudely awakened by a call this morning asking if I knew where you were because they couldn't find Skye. Seems she left without letting them know where she was going, and they were worried about her." Camden ran his fingers through his hair. It was almost time for a trim. "Uncle John helped us figure out where you were."

"My dad knew where I was today?"

"Your dad knows a lot more about you than you give him credit for." Camden closed his eyes.

"I guess he was mad." Ryan's voice sounded much less cocky than it had earlier.

"Didn't seem to be. Looked like he pitied me having to clean it up with Bree and Katie though."

"Did Katie freak? Skye said she probably would." Ryan groaned. "Although you should've heard Skye freak when her car wasn't in the drive when we got back. It's like she thought they'd left without her. Instead, it sounds like they just went to the mountain anyway."

"Good. I suggested they should." Camden smiled to himself. And good for them for taking Skye's car too. That might teach her a lesson about ruining well-laid plans.

"She wasn't happy at all that they'd taken her vehicle though. Furious is more like it."

"What did she expect them to do? She knew the agenda for today. Did she think they'd just stay at Jodie's house and worry about her all day instead? That's not nice." Camden got off his couch and paced the length of his living room.

"I don't know what she thought, but she didn't think they'd drive her car since she wasn't there."

"Maybe she should've stayed with them if she wanted to drive." Camden leaned against his door and studied his boring backyard through the glass. How much work would it take to make it look more like Jodie's yard? Would Katie like something like that? Would Katie care after today? Despite what Bree had texted, he still wasn't sure.

"Did you at least go kiss your girl goodbye before you headed off without even bidding me adieu?" Ryan sounded neglected although Camden couldn't figure out why.

"You weren't even answering your phone. How was I supposed to let you know I was leaving?" Camden paced again, needing to let off some frustration. "And no. I didn't get to kiss Katie. When I went over to try and help calm her down, she basically told me I'd wasted my week because things weren't going to work between us."

"Ouch."

"Yeah. To say the least." Camden released a sigh. "I'm going to let her cool off again and then see if she's changed her mind, but I'm not sure anymore. Maybe it was too good to be true. I mean, it's not like we'd really gotten to know each other that much this week. Just enough to know there was attraction. She doesn't even know where I live."

"What?" Ryan laughed. "You never told her?"

"She never asked. The only reason I know where she lives is because her sister was teasing her about it." Camden picked at a spot on the countertop that divided his kitchen from the living area.

"Dude, you should've done what I suggested when you first approached her. Thrown her back." Ryan was probably shaking his head on his end of the conversation. "She's run you through the whole spectrum of emotions and craziness this week. Not worth it in my book."

"I suppose you prefer girls like Skye who aren't even worried about their friends enough to let them know they've made other plans for the day? Or who invite strangers to join their group instead of sticking with the original plan of a girls' week?" Camden lightly hit his fist against the granite.

"Skye and I had fun together this week, but that's all there was to it. Neither of us went in with any expectations beyond that." Ryan was suddenly more serious than Camden had ever heard him. "I'm not like you, Cam. I don't know if I'll ever settle down and find someone to spend forever with. But I definitely know I'm not ready for that any time soon. Neither is Skye."

"I wondered if there was anything more serious than a road trip fling going on. I should've known better."

"It's not a sin not to be ready to grow up, you know."

"I never said it was." Camden rubbed between his eyes to release the stress building there. "But I will say that someday you're going to have to, ready or not. And the sooner you accept that fact, the easier it will be."

"I'm not accepting anything until I absolutely have to."

So much for Camden being a good influence. "I pity you then."

"Save your pity for someone else. I'm doing just fine." Ryan's voice ground through the phone. "Not everyone has to turn out like you to be okay. Did you know that? You might have more fun if you'd relax a little and realize not everything has to have eternal consequences."

Camden pressed his lips together, trapping a snarky comeback behind them. No point arguing when Ryan got like this. Life wasn't supposed to be a competition, but Ryan hadn't realized it yet. Best to just leave things as they were.

"Listen, thanks for letting me hang out this week. The trip was fun. I appreciate your dad inviting me." Camden stared out his back door again.

"Yeah. I'm not sure you had that much fun, but I know I did. It was definitely interesting."

"Definitely." Camden pictured where flower beds might go. And a swing set. "I'll talk to you again soon, okay?"

"Sure. Glad you got home all right."

"I did. Bye."

Ryan didn't even answer. The phone went silent, and Camden tossed it onto the couch. He couldn't worry about his cousin right now. He had a future to plan.

---

Skye's voice reached Katie's ears the moment she pushed open her sister's door. "I can't believe they just drove off with my car! What were they thinking? What if they had a wreck or something? It's not even in their name. If that car has a dent or scratch anywhere on it—"

"It doesn't." Bree's voice cut through Skye's tirade. "I was very careful. I even parked as far away from people as I could just to make sure it would be less likely for your precious convertible to be hurt. And if you didn't want us to take it without you, maybe you should've stuck with the original plans for today instead of making your own."

Jodie pointed to all three of them. "Look, I don't care how you work this out, but you need to do it as quietly as possible. Riley's only been asleep for an hour, and if you wake him up, I'll beat y'all."

Jodie had always been able to pull off a good "mom" face. Katie set her purse on the table by the door and kicked off her shoes. Her legs reminded her that she'd done more climbing today than ... well, than ever. She followed Bree's lead and moved to Jodie's comfortable sofa.

"Where did you go, anyway?" Skye's voice was lower now. Evidently Jodie's threat had not fallen on deaf ears.

"Stone Mountain. Just like we said." Bree propped her feet up on the coffee table. "There was a great view. I mean, we couldn't see all the way to Six Flags or anything, but still ..."

"You knew where I went?" Skye crossed her arms.

"Riley overheard you talking to Ryan yesterday. He figured out you were headed to ride coasters." Katie tucked her legs underneath her.

"So, you didn't worry at all?" Skye's pout didn't endear her to Katie whatsoever.

"Oh, we worried. After all, you set off the house alarm and woke up Nick. Then you drove off with Ryan with no word as to why you were leaving, who you were going with, or where you were headed. Camden didn't know anything about it either. Thankfully, between Riley's memory and the tracker Ryan's dad had on his phone, we put the clues together and figured things out. I mean, it's not like you left a note or answered any of your calls or texts."

"Ryan's dad tracks him?"

"I think it's sort of like the app we use to keep up with each other." Bree held up her phone. "Of course, I couldn't use it on you because I guess you had your phone off."

"I dropped it in the ocean earlier this week, and it hasn't dried out yet." Skye pulled a bag of rice from her purse. The corner of her cell peeked out from behind several grains.

"You didn't have it yesterday?" Katie couldn't imagine Skye going more than ten minutes without her device.

"No. I think I'm going through withdrawals." Skye slumped down into the recliner. "I didn't even think about the fact that you couldn't call me. I mean, Ryan had his phone."

"He wasn't answering either, evidently."

They sat for several minutes in silence.

"I'm surprised Camden wasn't with you today. I guess I figured he'd give you a ride." Skye picked at a frayed spot on her shorts.

"Camden went home." Katie heard more hurt in her voice than she wanted.

"Home? Where?"

"I don't know. I never asked him. I was too mad and riled up this morning to be decent to anyone, and I basically threw away everything we'd gained this week." Katie swallowed a lump of disappointment from her throat. She would not cry about this. It wasn't worth it.

"You did what?" Skye leaned forward to study Katie, then pointed at Bree. "Why didn't you do something?"

"Me? What was I supposed to do? It was taking everything Jodie and I could think of to keep Katie from imploding. Her worry over you went to anger just like that!" Bree snapped. "Evidently she's been bottling up quite a lot of emotions over not only this week but several years. And something tells me you have too."

"Me?" Skye pressed both hands to her chest. "You know I don't keep my emotions inside."

"And yet you ditched us to hang with Ryan almost the whole week after being so excited to take this one last trip together before my wedding." Bree tapped her chin. "I think maybe Katie isn't the only one upset about me getting married."

Skye crossed her arms and leaned back. "You must be joking. I'm the one who introduced you to Nathan in the first place. Of course I'm thrilled to see the match I made working out so well."

"Oh really?" Bree leaned forward. "So you're avoiding spending time with the girls who are supposed to be your best friends because …?"

Skye stood again and began to pace the area in front of the television. "Look. I didn't mean to ditch you guys. But once I started hanging out with Ryan, I figured it made sense. I mean, he and I both knew we were just in it to have some fun this week. And we all know that after your wedding we'll probably never really spend any time together again. Might as well cut the cords sooner rather than later, right?"

Bree jumped up and caught Skye in a hug. "We're going to spend as much time together as we can work out. Maybe we can do a girls' weekend every few years. Or visit whenever we pass in the direction one of the others lives. But we don't have to cut each other out of our lives if we don't want to. Especially with social media and texting. We can still keep up."

"No." Skye shook her head. "It's not going to happen. You're going to marry Nathan and go off to live your happily ever after. And Katie is off to work her dream job. And she'll probably find someone to marry soon too. I'm not ready for any of that. Where does any of this leave me?"

"If it makes you feel any better, I probably *won't* get married any time soon." Katie shook her head. "Not if I treat every guy the way I did Camden this morning."

"Why'd you do it, Katie? Why did you chase him off?" Skye pulled from Bree's arms and plopped down beside Katie.

"Maybe I'm scared too." Katie twisted her fingers in her lap. "I mean, it's a lot of change all at once."

"And we all know you don't handle change well." Skye leaned her head on Katie's shoulders. "But you could probably learn."

"Well, I for one wish I'd known you were both so upset over me marrying Nathan." Bree slumped in front of them. "Maybe we should postpone the wedding."

"No!" Skye shouted.

They both pulled Bree until she landed between them.

"No." Katie poked Bree in the shoulder. "You're ready to be married. Just because we're not doesn't mean you shouldn't go forward with your plans. Besides Nathan would kill us if he had to wait any longer. You've already been engaged for a year."

"Tell me about it." Bree's voice was full of exasperation.

"See? You're ready too." Skye shook her head. "Don't let us hold you back."

"And we've got all day tomorrow and tomorrow night at my place to soak up the last of our road trip. And then a few days around the wedding too. It's not like this is goodbye forever." Bree glanced back and forth between the girls. "Although if we don't get to bed and get some sleep, none of us is going to be fit to drive that car all the way back to Memphis tomorrow."

"True." Skye pushed up and yawned. "I was up way too early."

"And whose fault is that?" Bree bumped Skye out of the way as she started toward the hallway. "Not ours. It's your fault we were up almost as early. Not the other way around."

"Coming Katie?" Skye looked over her shoulder.

"In a minute. I might do some stretches out here to see if I can keep my legs from getting any tighter."

The girls nodded and headed into the room they'd been sharing. Katie moved to the floor and leaned over one leg then the other, resting her head against her shins. She breathed in and out, willing peace and relaxation through her body as she stretched.

"I think that's the only thing I'm jealous of." Jodie's voice above her pulled Katie out of her zone.

"What?" Katie sat up and bent her legs criss-cross style.

"Being able to get on the floor like that." Jodie pointed to the rug Katie occupied. "I'd love to be able to get down so easily. Riley always wants me to play, but we have to do it at the table so I can reach."

Jodie's words shot a knife through Katie's heart. Despite their talk earlier, the guilt she'd carried for years still clung to her. Sometimes she even dreamed the wreck happened all over again—but this time the driver hit her. She'd wake up unable to move her legs for several moments because of how real it all seemed. She rubbed her hands down her thighs. Had Jodie changed her mind about whose fault it all was?

"Don't do that." Jodie leaned over and swatted Katie.

"What?"

"Take all that guilt back on your shoulders. There's nothing any of us could have done. It falls fully on the shoulders of that idiot who drank too much and then got behind the wheel. If he hadn't made that choice, he wouldn't have hit our car while we were looking at Christmas lights." Jodie shook her head. "But I want to know more about something you mentioned earlier. Tell me about your panic attacks."

Katie pulled her knees up to her chest and hugged them. "What do you want to know?"

"I didn't realize you were still having them, for one thing. Do you know what triggers them?"

"Alcohol." Katie spit the word out.

"Drinking it?" Jodie leaned forward, a frown wrinkling her whole face.

"You know me better." Katie pushed to her feet.

"Then tell me. Explain what you mean." Jodie followed her in the wheelchair.

"Every time that smell hits me, I'm right back to that night. Can't you remember?"

"I was knocked out. Remember?"

How could she forget?

"What happened while I was knocked out, Katie?"

Katie took a deep breath, bracing herself to dive back into the memories. And moment-by-moment, she told her sister what had happened after their wreck. And why it still haunted her, leading to the panic attacks.

"Katie, have you had any counseling for this?" Jodie's question pulled Katie's eyes open again.

"No. I keep hoping I'll grow out of it." Katie sank back onto the sofa again. "I mean, it's been so long."

"But it's obviously still bothering you." Jodie rolled up beside her. "And I think maybe this is effecting you more than just when you smell alcohol. Pretty sure this is why you're so concerned with having control over things. I mean, being in a wreck like that is basically the opposite of having control over your situation. That's why it's so hard for you to accept it when things don't go exactly the way you planned. But, Katie, that's not healthy. And it's going to hurt your relationships in the future too."

"You mean like how I ruined one this morning?" Katie put her head in her hands.

"Are you sure you've completely ruined it?"

"How could my meltdown not have ruined it?" Katie lifted her face enough to give her sister a skeptical look. "I mean, I told him following me and trying to get to know me all week was a mistake. How could I be so mean? And after taking me to the Braves game last night."

"Have you apologized?"

"How do I? I mean, I can't exactly promise I won't go crazy like that again. I'm not really known for keeping my head whenever something doesn't go my way." Katie shook her head.

"Which is why I think it's past time for you to seek help for this." Jodie leaned forward and pulled her sister into a hug. "I love you to the ends of the earth, but you've been fighting this by yourself for too long. When you get settled and find a church home, maybe they can recommend a good Christian counselor to help you get past this."

"I don't even know how I'm going to find somewhere to worship. I'm so bad at putting myself out there, meeting new people."

"I can help with that." Bree stood in the doorway in her pink-striped pajamas.

"How?" Katie shot her friend a confused look. "You've never lived in the Germantown area either.

"No, but I have a friend there and got a suggestion for where we can try this Sunday." Bree smiled as if she knew something more than just a good place to worship.

"Who's your friend?"

"Let's just say, I think you'll approve." Bree winked.

"Bree, you better not be trying to set me up with someone else just because things didn't work out with Camden." Katie shook a finger at her best friend.

"No worries. I know how you feel about being set up." Bree crossed her heart.

Katie wasn't so sure, but if her friend wanted to help her find a new church home, who was she to complain? New situations were not her thing, and having Bree around for the next few weeks was a relief. What she'd do after that, she had no idea.

# 17

"I can't do this. What was I thinking?" Katie flopped on the couch with a dramatic sigh. "I'm no good at meeting new people. Or making decisions. Why isn't there a way to just bring the church we've been worshiping at for four years with us? I was comfortable there. I knew what to expect. And everyone accepted me already, so I didn't have to worry about making a good impression."

Bree grabbed her arm and tugged until she relented and stood again. "Go brush your teeth. You look great. That skirt has always been one of my favorites of yours."

Katie ran her fingers down her floral-print skirt and smoothed her boho-style blouse. The mirror showed what it always did. At least one or two curls going the opposite directions of all the others, a nose too narrow, lips too wide, and eyes that were just there. What had Camden said about them? Something about them changing color depending on her shirt and mood. They did look bluer today, maybe because of the aquamarine in her top?

It didn't matter what he thought of her eyes. She'd probably never cross paths with him again ... except in her dreams. Those, she seemed to have no control over. And even if she did see him, he most likely wanted nothing to do with her after her insanity Friday morning. She needed to face facts. She'd chased off the one guy in the world who thought her eyes were amazing.

"Are you ready now?" Bree banged on the bathroom door. "We're going to be late."

"Good. Then we can sneak in the back and not as many people will see us." Katie muttered it under her breath.

"You know the back rows fill up quickly. The later we are, the less likely to get a seat near the back." Bree chided through the wood. This apartment needed thicker doors.

"Why did I want you to stay with me until the wedding?" Katie came out and stuck her tongue out at her best friend.

"Because you love me." Bree grabbed her arm and the Bibles and dragged her toward the door. "And because you'd never work up the nerve to do this otherwise. Let's go."

Skye wasn't leaving until after lunch to head the rest of the way to St. Louis, so she snuggled into the backseat. "Come on, Katie. How hard can it be? This is church we're talking about."

The building wasn't very far from where she lived. They had to drive only a few streets over. That was a definite perk. Bree pulled into a parking space and scanned the lot as if looking for someone.

"Was your friend supposed to meet us?" Katie played with the edge of her Bible.

"Not sure. Let's go in. I'm sure it won't be hard to find where we need to go." Bree led the way up the sidewalk and through the glass doors. People milled around the foyer, steering children down various hallways to classrooms, chatting and catching up with each other.

Katie swallowed a tremor of nervousness. She'd make a

fool of herself somehow this morning, and then these people would never want her here, even if she liked it. It was just too much change all at once. She'd get settled into her new home and job for a few weeks, and then maybe she'd try to find a church home again.

That made more sense. No one actually found a place to worship their first Sunday in a new town, right? She started to back toward the door once more when a familiar head across the foyer caught her eye. She froze.

"Katie? What's wrong?" Skye craned her head as if to try and follow the direction of Katie's sight. "You look as though you've seen a ghost."

"He's here!" Katie grabbed Bree and Skye and pulled them behind a pillar. "What is he doing here? He can't live around here. There's no way. It would be too much of a coincidence."

"Who?" Skye tried to peek around the column, but Katie jerked her back.

"Camden." Katie turned her back and rubbed a hand across her forehead. "*Serendipity* and *coincidence* are just words. Things like that don't happen in real life. Did he follow me? He can't track me just because he has my number, right?"

"Katie." Bree squeezed her arm. "He's the friend who told me about this congregation."

Where had all the air gone? Why couldn't she draw a full breath? Bree? Bree had coordinated with him to get her here today? Bree had betrayed her?

"You set me up." Katie's voice came out hurt and confused. "He lives here?"

"Somewhere near here, I guess. He didn't tell me. Just said this would be a good fit for you." Bree shrugged and glanced over her shoulder. "But you'd better calm down quickly, because I think he spotted us."

"No. I'm not staying. I can't." Katie stepped toward the

door one more time and ran right into Camden's chest. His arms automatically clasped hers as she rocked on her feet. She looked up into his blue eyes and saw an expression she couldn't fully read. Hope? Excitement? Something else?

"Fancy meeting you here." One corner of his lips tugged up in that adorable smile of his. "I told you we'd run into each other again. And you were sure Tennessee was too long a state for our paths to cross."

"You live here?" Katie realized he still held her arms and quickly took a step back.

"At the church building? Some weeks it feels like it, but no. I live in Collierville, just a few miles down the road." He hooked a thumb over his shoulder.

"We live that close to each other? How did you find out where I live?" Katie shook her head. "Jodie. Jodie let it slip the other day. I'd hoped you hadn't heard her. And then when you said Tennessee, I guess I just imagined you were somewhere near Nashville or something. At least this confirms why your area code looked so familiar. It's a Memphis one. Same as the library's."

"You're rambling." Bree whispered in her ear.

Her lips clamped shut.

"Nice to see you again, Camden."

"Thanks for helping get her here." Camden shot a real smile at both Skye and Bree. "We're about to start Sunday school. Would you like to join me in the class I attend? It's mostly made up of people around our age."

"Sounds great." Bree gave a thumbs up. "Lead the way."

Walking down the hall, his hand lightly touched the small of her back as he guided them through the last few stragglers. The classroom had chairs lined up facing the opposite wall, but all the seats in the back were taken, and he walked up to the second row.

Katie swallowed a lump of nerves and tried to ignore all the eyes she was sure were directed at her. She started to sit in a chair two away from Camden, but Skye pushed her on to the seat right next to his. Lowering herself slowly, she kept her back straight, her shoulders stiff. She wouldn't let herself touch him any more than normal.

Why wasn't he mad at her? Why had he arranged this? She hadn't left him with any kind of hope, yet he'd gone out of his way to make sure he could see her again. And how did he and Bree communicate, anyway? Her thoughts were interrupted by the teacher clearing his throat at the lectern.

"Camden, I see you have some visitors today. Can you introduce them to us?"

Words Katie never wanted to hear. She willed the fire creeping into her cheeks to slow down, but it listened as well as her meddling friends. Her fingers clenched around her Bible until she was sure there'd be an imprint by the time she let go.

"This is Katie, Skye, and Bree. We met earlier this week when our vacations crossed paths, and when I found out Katie was moving to this area, I invited them to join us for services this morning." Camden's voice was calm and displayed none of the hurricane of emotions whirling through her.

"Welcome! We're glad to have you ladies with us today, and, Katie, we hope you consider making this your church home." The teacher moved on to prayer requests, and some of the tension slid out of her shoulders with the attention of the class focused elsewhere.

"Everyone here will love you. You don't have to look so stressed out and worried." Camden's whisper in her ear sent a shiver down her spine and accelerated her heartrate.

"You can't know that." She kept her voice as low as his though she refused to be as intimate and get so near him.

"I can know that. Because I'm already most of the way

there, and the rest of the class is much less picky about who they love."

She darted a glance at him, eyes wide, but his head faced forward as if the discussion of someone's new baby was the most interesting thing in the world. If she hadn't been watching him so intently, she'd have missed the slight twitch at the edge of his mouth, the tiny crinkles around his eyes as he held back a smile. She faced forward, too, swallowing a huge knot of emotions.

The snippets of the class discussion that crept through her foggy brain seemed good, but she wasn't sure. She couldn't convince her mind to focus on anything beyond Camden's words. Even after all she'd done the previous week, her crazy outbursts, awful panic attacks, and uncontrollable anger, her quirks and her stubbornness and her impulsive kiss on the beach—despite all that, he still wanted her here and admitted he was halfway to loving her. How could that be?

"Camden, introduce us to your friends." Two pretty girls came up after class was over, smiling and extending hands to shake. "Camden never pays any attention to girls, so when he walked in this morning with three, we figured you must be relatives of some kind."

He never paid any attention to girls? But he'd given her almost devoted attention all week. And she wasn't nearly as attractive as these two.

"Nope. Not relatives. New friends from vacation." Camden gave the introductions again. "Katie here is going to be the newest librarian in Germantown."

"Oh! I bet that's a fun job." The brunette giggled. "I never have much time to read, but I sometimes think it would be fun."

"I can't imagine not reading." Katie shrugged. "It got me

through high school when no one wanted anything to do with me, that's for sure." Why had she blurted that out?

"Really? No one wanted anything to do with you? But you're so cute." The redhead cocked her head at an angle and frowned. "They must've been crazy. You stick with us, Katie. We'll show you all the best places to shop and eat. And once a month, we do a girls' night where we watch a chick flick and eat until we absolutely can't take another bite. Ooh! And you've got to sign up to come on ladies' retreat with us this fall. It's so fun. I'm Stella, by the way."

Katie opened and closed her mouth, unsure what to say to all that.

"Told you." Camden's words tickled the hair at the edge of her ear.

She followed them all to the auditorium for worship in a bit of a daze. They liked her already? They didn't even know her yet. Had Camden set that up too? Surely not. Especially after everything ...

"I like this place, Katie." Bree leaned over and whispered before services started. "I think Camden's right. It looks like a great fit for you."

---

What Camden would give to know what was going through Katie's head! She'd been completely baffled by Stella's exuberance earlier. That had been easy to see. But he couldn't quite get a read on how she felt about him living so close. Was she happy? Angry? Confused?

He tucked his ponderings away for later. Right now, his thoughts were supposed to be on God. He sent up a silent prayer that Katie would accept this for what it was meant to be —an opportunity to start fresh and hopefully see where this might go—as well as a chance to find an amazing church family on her first weekend in town. Camden didn't know what he'd do without this congregation who'd welcomed him with open arms. He knew they'd do the same for her, if she'd let them.

He opened his Bible and tried to follow along with the preacher, but the glances she sent his way over and over again distracted him. A couple more songs, with her alto voice singing softly beside him, and then time for the closing prayer. Camden wove his fingers through hers automatically. She stiffened and then relaxed enough that he didn't feel obligated to pull away.

"A friend, huh, Camden?" Patricia's voice teased as she and Stella made their way out of the pew behind them after the service. "You've never held our hands during a prayer."

Katie's cheeks blushed, and she tugged her fingers free.

"I'd love to invite you all to lunch." Camden looked between Katie and her friends.

"I need to hit the road pretty fast to make it home by when my father thinks I should get there." Skye shrugged. "Otherwise, I'd totally take you up on that. And if Katie turns you down, Cam, you get my number from her, okay? I still need to find a date to Bree's wedding."

"You're kidding, right?" Bree playfully punched Skye's arm. "Because that's beyond not cool."

"What? If Katie wants to throw something that good away, it's her loss." Skye's voice faded as they headed up the aisle, leaving Katie and him behind.

"Maybe I can get a raincheck on lunch." He started to reach out to squeeze her arm, then pulled back.

"Is this about the money?"

Katie's words caught him off guard. What was she talking about?

"I still have it, but it's at home. On my dresser. I didn't realize you'd … that we'd be seeing you …" Katie shook her head. "Anyway, I'll get it to you as soon as I can. You shouldn't have left it in the first place."

"Left it?" Oh. The gas money Uncle John had given him. "It's no big deal. Just some cash my uncle handed me before I left that morning. I didn't need it."

"It is a big deal. Maybe you're used to throwing away hundred-dollar bills, but I definitely am not. That's a lot of money, Camden." She fiddled with the ribbon on her Bible. "I'll get it back to you."

"This wasn't about the money." He crooked a finger under her chin to lift her head so he could look into her amazing eyes. "I don't care about the money. I just wanted a chance to see you again. When Bree texted me the other day, I came up with a plan to make that happen. I didn't want … I didn't want Friday morning to be our final note. Honestly, I'm not sure I want us to end on any note. I want to get to know you better."

"You must be a sucker for punishment." Katie turned her head away again. "I showed you all sorts of bad sides last week."

"And all sorts of good ones too."

"Thanks for suggesting a place to worship, Camden. It was really nice." Katie started to move past him. "And I'll get your money to you soon."

"Katie." He caught her arm, held it just tight enough for her to know he hoped she'd stay another moment. "Please. You … I …"

She let her gaze land on him, curiosity written all over her lovely face.

He couldn't let her go again. "Tell you what—I'll take the money back on one condition."

A frown creased her brow, wariness filling her features.

"I'll take it back only if I can use it to take you on a date." He lifted an eyebrow, waiting for her to protest.

"A hundred-dollar date? Where on earth would you take me that would cost that much? I'm used to matinees and fast food. Not some fancy place that would cost more than my bridesmaid dress."

"You like baseball ..." He snapped his fingers. "We have the Redbirds downtown."

"No. I like Braves baseball. I don't really care for any other team." She shook her head.

"So, you're not really a baseball fan then?"

"I like baseball. But only the Braves. I can't work up the excitement for anyone else for some reason. I know it sounds funny." She twisted her toe into the carpet.

"What about playing? We have a church softball league here." He couldn't resist, even though he had a feeling he knew what her reaction would be.

"Oh, no! No. I ... well, this is totally embarrassing, but I can't ever hit the ball because ... well, because I cringe and jerk back every time it comes at me. I can't get over the fear of it colliding with my arm or head instead of the bat." She wrinkled her nose.

"Seems like a legitimate fear. Okay." He tapped his fingers against his pants leg as he ran through options in his head. A commercial he'd seen the night before came to mind. Perfect! "What about a play?"

"A play?"

"You strike me as the kind of girl who'd like a musical. Am I right?"

"And if I'm not?" She donned a saucy look, as if challenging him to like her anyway. Challenge accepted.

"I think you are." He smiled. "And I have the perfect opportunity to find out. If you decide to give me that money back. Up to you."

"Katie, are you coming?" Skye waved from the doorway. "I've got to go."

"I need to leave." Katie took a few steps down the aisle.

"Let me know when and where, Katie." Camden crossed his arms. "I look forward to it."

Was it smart to leave the ball in her court? In this case he wasn't sure, but the deed was done. She'd be the one to determine whether he got another date with her. If she found a way to return the money quickly, the Orpheum was showing a performance he was certain would be right up her alley. If she waited too long, there were always other things to do. Could he sit back and wait? That was a whole other issue.

# 18

One word. That's all the text said when Camden saw the message from Katie on Monday morning. But it was enough to send his heart soaring. He reread the text.

Okay.

She was willing to go on another date.

He hadn't replied. Couldn't. He wanted to see her in person. All through his PRN hours at the assisted living center, he'd had to refocus on the task at hand. His patients deserved his undivided attention on performing their stretches correctly. His brain kept returning to a girl with soft brown curls and passionate hazel eyes.

Unfortunately, he was asked to work a couple extra hours because someone else had called in sick that morning. The afternoon stretched on until he wasn't sure he'd make it through his last few therapy sessions. He slowly straightened Mrs. Pozowski's leg and gave her a grin.

"All right, Mrs. P. You're all done for today. Is it getting any easier?"

"I don't know, dear. These old bones just don't do like they used to." She held out a hand and let him ease her to a sitting position. "Getting old isn't all it's cracked up to be."

"Well, if I have to get old, I hope I do it as gracefully as you." He squeezed her fingers before turning to pack up his bag.

"You're a sweetheart. Someone better snatch you up fast." She shook her head and straightened her blouse. "Although you're a terrible liar."

He laughed and bid her goodbye before walking down the sticky hallway to the front desk. "All done for today. Here's the paperwork. Call me if anything looks wrong, but I think it's all there."

"It usually is when you're the one turning it in, Camden." May Ellen turned from her computer screen and accepted the stack he held out. "If only all our PTs were as good as you."

"You just say that so I won't quit." He threw her a wink.

"Ha!" She shook her head, her braids bouncing with each turn. "You should have seen what a mess everything was in last week while you were away. No, sir. I mean it when I say I wish they were all like you."

"Well, hang on until Wednesday. That's the next time I'm scheduled to be here." He waved and walked out into the hot summer-like afternoon.

Freedom at last. Not that he minded his PRN work. It gave him a little extra cushion of money each month, and he adored helping the older patients recover some of their lost muscle use. But on a day like today, when he was itching to find out more about that message from Katie, he was more than glad to be done.

He had no idea what her schedule was, but at three in the afternoon, surely she'd be around the library still. They didn't close until nine. Even if she was working the late shift, she should be there by now, right?

Only one way to find out.

He even had a backup excuse for coming today. One of his coworkers had him hunting down extra copies of a how-to on strength training for the team. Camden planned to check the used bookstore inside. He parked, did a little drumbeat on his steering wheel, and walked up the path and into the coolness of the building. He paused in the doorway and breathed in the smell of old books. The hushed sounds of quiet conversations and riffling pages was a soothing music all its own.

With no idea which section she might be in and not spying her curls behind the main counter, he wandered shelf by shelf. Her pretty smile was nowhere in fiction or biographies. There, though. A familiar head dipping down to replace a book on a shelf in the how-to section. Her red top shimmered despite the shadowy light between shelves, and her red-and-blue-checked capris hugged her hips perfectly.

He made his way over the carpet, stopping right behind her as she paused to pull a paperback off her cart and return it to its home. "How's my favorite librarian today?"

She squealed and then covered her mouth, glancing around as if hoping no one had heard her. "You scared me!"

"That wasn't my intent." He held his hands out, palms up, to show he meant no harm.

"What on earth are you doing here?" She moved back to her stack and pulled another tome to place. This time, though, the shelf was too high, and even her tiptoes weren't enough for her to reach.

He grabbed the volume and slipped it into the right spot. "I wanted to talk to you, but I didn't want to text. I wanted to see you. To see if you really meant that message this morning the way it sounded."

"Oh." She absentmindedly flipped the edge of another book. "You wanted your money back."

"No." He leaned down and caught her gaze, relishing the beauty of her eyes. "I wanted to see you. To let you know how happy your text made me this morning."

She blinked and then put the paper-bound series on cooking chicken where it belonged amidst the other culinary how-tos. "I'm sort of working right now."

"When do you get off?" He leaned against the shelf. "I don't want to get you in trouble on your first day."

"Five. I've been here since eight."

"Meet me at the park when you're done?" He pointed out the window to the playground and benches nearby.

"I don't have the money with me, Camden." She looked down, at the books, anywhere but at him.

"I'm not asking for money. I'm asking for you to come meet me for a little while after you get off." He grabbed her fingers and squeezed. "Please."

"All right." She nodded. "See you in a bit."

He walked away and didn't care one whit that there was an extra bounce to his step. Though he obviously had some work to do to convince her this was going to work. Despite all they'd been through last week, she remained skittish and uncertain. Would his plan be enough?

It had to be. He couldn't stand it otherwise. After checking through the bookstore and not finding a copy of the book he needed, he headed down the road to his favorite barbecue joint. Maybe some pulled pork would help her open up. And if she'd been at work as long as she said she had, she was sure to be hungry.

She hadn't looked thrilled about seeing him the day before. Had come across as rather betrayed, actually. Still … she'd sent that text this morning. That had to count for something, right?

While he waited on a bench near the playground, he sent up prayers. As interested as he was in Katie, he knew there were still issues to work through. Would she trust him enough to open up? Would she trust herself enough to give this more than half a chance?

*Please, God, let it be so.*

---

Katie shook her hands out at her sides as she stepped out of the cool library and into the hot afternoon sunshine. Her fingers still shook slightly. She pulled her bag's strap farther up on her shoulder and shaded her eyes to see if she could find the bench where Camden wanted to meet. It didn't take long to notice his spiky blond hair. He sat, hunched over a bit, head bowed, his back to her, in the shade of a tall oak tree.

Deep breath in, deep breath out. She could do this. She'd spent most of the previous week with him. Why the butterflies in her tummy now?

Because this wasn't vacation. There was no end date to make this seem like a temporary fling. Instead, potential glimmered at the edges, just the way sunlight gleamed in his hair. Was she ready for that? Was he seriously interested in her with all her problems? She shook her head. Too good to be true, just like this whole thing had been. He was probably just trying to find a way to break things off with her.

She reached the bench and realized he was praying. For a way to let her down easy? For wisdom and peace as he talked to someone with a ridiculously short fuse? For—?

"You're here." His voice broke into her thoughts and pulled her back to the present. "I picked up some barbecue. I figured you'd be hungry."

"That sounds amazing, actually." She slid onto the seat on the far end. No need to sit closer than necessary.

He passed her a Styrofoam container that leaked amazing smells of smoky meat and vinegar-based sauce. She opened the lid and inhaled, her eyes closed. The sandwich was nestled in a bed of curly fries, and she quickly stuffed one in her mouth.

"Root beer?" He held out a cup, a grin playing on those irresistible lips.

"Thanks." She took a long sip, embarrassed he'd caught her stuffing her face so shamelessly. Not that he hadn't seen her eat before. But this time had been more … slovenly. "Sorry I didn't wait for you."

"It's okay. I feel the same way about their fries. Go ahead and enjoy before they get soggy." He leaned back and opened his own container. "They have the best sauce I've ever had too."

"So, Memphis barbecue really is as great as people say it is?" She took a big bite of her pulled pork and let out a happy sigh. "Yeah. That's good."

Camden laughed and took a drink. "I like it. I mean, it's not the Rendezvous, but I can't afford to eat there every week. This place is a little more reasonable. And a lot closer."

"You're wearing scrubs." She studied the way the blue of his outfit brought out the color of his eyes. "I thought you said you worked as an assistant football coach."

"I worked at the assisted living center this morning." He chewed a fry for a moment. "I don't get to put in as many hours during the school year, but I pick up extra shifts during the summer break when others are on vacation. It gives me a little extra money each month to put back for home improvement projects and things like that."

"So, you really are a physical therapist." She leaned back

and let her gaze rest on him. "It sounded real when you told me last week, but I was also wondering if you weren't trying to impress me and gain my trust by making it up."

"I'm not that kind of guy." He turned to face her more fully. "If I can't show a girl the real me and have her still interested, then it's not worth it. I want a relationship where both of us can be ourselves, flaws and all."

"I definitely have some flaws." She pinched a fry into pieces. "I guess I turned out to be the beast in this relationship, huh?"

"Does that make me the beauty?"

She glanced back up and had to chuckle at the smirk on his face. "I'm not going to help you get a big head."

"Katie." He laid a hand on top of hers. "You're not a beast. You struggle with things, sure. But that doesn't mean you're awful. Everyone has problems."

She shook her head. "But most people can control their temper enough to keep themselves from chasing off a guy who stirred up all kinds of amazing feelings in them. I mean, I was more than surprised you wanted to have anything to do with me after what I said at Jodie's."

"I also know you didn't really mean it."

"How can you know that?" She lifted her hands and tossed his off. "How can you know that much about me after only a week? I don't understand."

"In one week, I've seen you under duress, frustrated, tired, exhilarated, peaceful, happy, competitive, shy, and maybe even attracted. And I've seen the way you've handled each and every one of the emotions. Yes. You blew your top on Friday. But you also realize it now. And that means you're less likely to go that far next time." He sat back and took another bite of his dinner.

She quietly munched some more fries while she considered all he'd said. He'd seen almost the whole spectrum of emotions in one week. And he still sat beside her, wanting to go on a date, spend time together, maybe more. Was he for real?

"Did you want to hear my idea for a date?" His question pulled her from her mulling.

"I'm almost afraid." She closed the lid of her mostly empty box, surprised she'd eaten as much as she had.

"I think you're the only girl I've ever met who didn't want to know where a guy might like to take her." He scooted a bit closer. "You're not the tiniest bit curious?"

"Maybe this much." She held up her finger and thumb less than an inch apart.

"I'll take it." He rested his arm across the back of the bench and leaned nearer still. "I'll give you a clue."

She raised an eyebrow but offered no more encouragement.

"It's a performance about a librarian."

"A librarian?" She frowned. "What kind of performance?"

"A musical. At the Orpheum." One corner of his mouth tipped up. "Can you guess?"

"A musical about a librarian?"

"Mm hmm."

She leaned back and felt his arm against her shoulders. Her body and heart argued with each other. Part of her wanted to believe this thing growing between them was real, but the other part couldn't trust it yet.

"Give up?" His voice pulled her back once more.

"Okay. I give up."

"*The Music Man*." He leaned forward to look in her eyes. "What do you think?"

She loved that play. How had he known? Had Bree let it slip?

"What's wrong?" He ran a finger down her cheek. "Do you hate musicals after all? I thought you were just kidding."

"I love them." She ducked her head as she whispered the words. "It's perfect."

"So, you'll go? Wait. What's your schedule for the next few weeks? Do you know yet?"

"For now, I'm going to work from open until five most days. It might change in the future, but I requested Sundays off as much as possible." She fiddled with a loose thread on the edge of her shirt.

"That would work well if your schedule stays the same. We could go grab a bite to eat first. Maybe even at the Rendezvous." He tucked one of her curls behind her ear. "Then an evening at the Orpheum watching Harold Hill win the heart of Marian, madam librarian."

"It sounds too good to be true. How did you know I'd love something like that?" She risked a glance his direction and found him much closer than before. Just a breath away.

"I didn't, really. But from everything else you've liked this week, I thought this might fit. I'm glad I was right." His finger traced her jaw, moved to the bottom of her lip.

Her chest tightened, her breath coming faster and shallower. "And you like musicals, do you?"

"I do, believe it or not." That corner of his mouth turned up once more. "I have two older sisters who made sure I was schooled in all of them."

"*You're* almost too good to be true, you know?" Her words came out as more of a whisper than anything.

"Even after hitting you in the head with a volleyball?"

She caught sight of his teasing smile right before he pressed his lips to hers. The kiss wasn't long, but it was full of emotion on both sides, of wanting and wishful thinking and hope.

"Maybe that volleyball hit me harder than I thought." She

rubbed the side of her head as they leaned back. "I keep thinking I'm living out a fairy tale."

"As long as it has a happily ever after, I don't mind." He wove his fingers through hers.

"That's rushing things just a bit. We haven't even been on a real date yet. We might find we have nothing in common ... besides liking musicals and the Braves."

He laughed. "You have a hard time letting yourself be happy, don't you?"

"You have no idea." She rose and started to pull her hand away.

"Then I look forward to finding out. I'll let you know about tickets and make sure that still works with your schedule." He tugged her closer again as he stood in front of her. "Patricia and Stella wanted me to tell you they're having girls' night this Friday, and they want you to come. I think they want to pump you for information about how we met."

"Tell them maybe next time." She shoved down the trepidation the thought of hanging out with new acquaintances always put in her heart.

"Come to Bible study with me Wednesday night and tell them yourself." He pressed his forehead to hers.

"Maybe."

"Please?"

"Okay. But you know Bree will come too. She's living with me until the wedding." Katie pulled back again. "In fact, she'll probably be worrying about me. She expected me home long before now."

"Bree is more than welcome. Just tell her I kidnapped you. She'll forgive your tardiness." He winked.

"You're that powerful, huh? Got my best friend hood-winked or something?" She couldn't stop the grin creeping over her lips.

"No. But she's the one who stole my number out of your phone so she could find a way to get us together after vacation." He kissed her forehead. "I think she's rooting for us."

"That traitor." Katie rolled her eyes and started walking to her car.

"Traitor or not, I'm glad she's on our side." He pulled her into one more hug before opening her door for her. "If she hadn't intervened, I might still be sitting at home, moping around and wondering if I'd ever get to see you again."

"Or you would've had more time to realize you'd narrowly escaped getting caught up with a crazy woman." She cranked the engine to start the air conditioner cooling the interior of her sedan.

"You're not crazy. Maybe you can explain why you think you are when we're on our date." He squeezed her fingers one more time before backing up.

"We'll see." She licked her lips. "Text me about Wednesday night so I don't forget."

"You got it." He held out a package of candy. "I got you these too. To help you remember me until we see each other again."

She took it from his hand, shaking her head. "Peanut butter ones, huh?"

"Did I remember right?"

"You did." One more way he was perfect to add to all the rest.

"Enjoy. I'll see you in a couple days."

He waved as she drove off. He wanted to know more about her craziness. It would either scare him off completely or he would prove he really was as amazing as he seemed. And she had little time to work up the nerve to talk about it.

# 19

"Are you sure it's safe down here?" Katie peered out the window as they neared downtown Memphis. The old warehouses and unkempt homes she spied from the interstate were less than encouraging. "Aren't there a lot of shootings?"

"We're not going to that part of the city." Camden glanced at her with a smirk. "And every city has shootings. Not just Memphis. They're really trying to rejuvenate downtown. There have been lots of restorations around the river. See?"

He maneuvered off the interstate and followed a street that wove parallel to the Mississippi. Upscale apartments winked at her from the other side. She relaxed a little and took it all in. After parking in a garage, he led her up the street and down an alley to an inconspicuous door. Inside, Katie breathed in the most amazing aromas she had ever discovered.

"Oh." Camden froze. "I forgot they serve alcohol here. And that they're rather known for their beer."

Only a slight flutter stirred Katie's heart. "I've eaten in restaurants where people were drinking before. It's not all drinking that bothers me. More the smell. Sort of hard to explain. With the scent of barbecue, I should be fine." She squeezed his hand.

Sitting at a red-checkered-cloth-covered table, they studied the plastic menus. She ran her finger along the prices. "That money from your uncle isn't going to cover this and the theater tickets too. It's too much."

His hand covered hers. "I've got it. Don't worry about it. I worked extra hours the last few weeks, remember?"

"But that money is supposed to be for your home improvement projects." She tried to pull her fingers free, but he clasped them tighter.

"Katie, it's okay. I promise. Because Uncle John's money covered the tickets, we can do this. No problem. Just pick out what sounds best. I recommend the ribs. But don't let any sauce get on that pretty dress of yours."

She unfolded a napkin in her lap over her simple black dress. It wasn't anything fancy, but the princess cut flattered her figure. She grinned and agreed to order what she wanted.

Licking sauce off her fingers an hour later, she looked up and caught his eye. "What?"

"You have something." He leaned over the table and swiped at the corner of her lip. "Here."

As if no time had passed, she was back beside the hotel pool in New Orleans or the fireplace in Gulf Shores, her heart pumping madly at the gentle touch of his fingers, her lips silently willing him to lean a little closer and kiss her already. His Adam's apple bobbed, and she suspected he was reliving the same memories.

"You seem to be good at catching me in that position." She grinned.

"I do, don't I?" He wiped his fingers on his napkin and leaned back. "You about ready to meander down the road again?"

"Sure." She set her napkin aside and rose, grateful for his hand around hers as they wound back through the crowded restaurant.

"We're a little early, but it's a nice evening for a stroll." He moved his hand to her waist and pulled her to his side as they walked down the sidewalk.

"It's a gorgeous evening. Almost a shame to spend it inside a theater." She relished the feel of his arm around her as they stood, waiting for a light to change.

"We're just down from AutoZone Park, if you'd rather go catch the game." He pointed over his shoulder with his thumb.

"I said *almost.*" She sent him a smirk and then walked alongside him again. "I don't think I'm really dressed for a baseball game."

"No." He shook his head. "That dress would be wasted in those seats. Just another couple blocks."

"Do you come down here very often?"

"Not really. It's more of a special-occasion thing. Sometimes a group from church gets together and comes over for an event. A baseball or basketball game. See? There's the basketball arena."

"There's a lot more down here than I realized." She drew her gaze away from people walking down the cross street. "Where are we?"

"This is Beale Street. The theater is just across there." He pointed to the other side of the intersection.

"Beale Street? Isn't that like Memphis's version of Bourbon Street?" Her heartrate accelerated more than she wished it would. She hadn't realized they'd be so close to a panic-attack-inducing location.

"They're similar. Both have great music, of course. But Beale is a little shorter and has a slightly different vibe." He gave her a gentle push to walk as the light changed for them to cross. "Why?"

"I just wasn't expecting to be so close ..."

"Oh." He stopped in the middle of the sidewalk and looked at her. "Are you okay? I know we just crossed the street, but we're seriously not going near that part of Beale Street unless you want to. I didn't even think about how close the theater was to that."

She focused her gaze on his eyes and willed her breathing to regain normality. "I'll be okay. As long as we don't have to get any closer."

"I promise. We'll even cross on the other side of the street when we head back to the car later." He pulled her to him, cradling her head to his chest, where his heart beat a rhythm faster than she expected. "Just tell me what I need to do."

"Let's just go on to the theater."

"All right." He led her up to the doors of the old building, the lights of the signs setting the entrance aglow. Into the carpeted foyer and up to the balcony where their seats were, his hand hovered just close enough to the small of her back that she was aware of it from her head to her toes. They settled into their plush seats, and she leaned forward to look toward the more expensive orchestra section and the stage below.

"It's a grand building, isn't it?"

"It was built back in the 20s, I think. And remodeled several times since. I keep thinking one of these years I'm going to buy season tickets, but I haven't yet." He flipped through his program.

"Oh, that would be fun." She leaned back and pointed to the advertisement for upcoming shows. "Look at all those great musicals coming next year."

"Is that what you want for Christmas?"

"Christmas? Good grief. It's not even June yet. I can't think that far ahead." Especially as she still wondered about the uncertainty of their relationship. Could it even last that long? More than six months. She wanted to tell him about her panic attacks ... about the reason for them. But she hadn't been able to bring it up during their walk.

"Gotta start shopping now if you want to find the best deals." He shot her a grin and then looked more serious. "What's wrong?"

"Wrong?" She tried to school her features back into a neutral or even excited expression, but she knew from his concerned look that she hadn't succeeded.

"You look worried. Are you still thinking about Beale Street?" He ran a finger down the side of her cheek.

"Sort of. I ... I wanted to tell you more about it. About why I can't handle ..."

"Excuse me." A couple stood on the other side of Camden and pointed to the seats beyond Katie. "We need to get through please."

"Of course." Camden stood and pulled her up so the others could get by.

The lights flickered overhead, warning people the show would begin soon. So much for having the conversation now. That's what she got for putting it off.

"We can talk later, okay? Whenever you're ready." He draped his arm over her shoulder and murmured the words directly in her ear. "No judging. No worries. But I'd love to understand more. To see if there's anything I can do to help."

She ducked her head. Could he read her heart? How else could he know so much of what was running through her mind? She nodded to let him know she'd heard. She didn't dare look at him.

The first notes of the orchestra reverberated throughout the house, and the actors appeared from behind the curtain, singing about *The Music Man*. She let herself relax as the songs carried her away to Iowa, where Harold Hill turned out to be exactly what the small town needed. Camden's arm pulled her a little closer, and she breathed in his spicy aftershave. He whispered some of the lyrics in her ear until she swatted him and told him to stop before the other patrons around them got upset.

Prince Charming, indeed. Not only did Camden live nearby, but also he liked musicals to the point of knowing the words? Bree would never believe this. How on earth had Katie stumbled into this relationship? Did things too good to be true have a chance to survive in the real world? Or would her panic attacks and uncontrollable temper drive him away?

Camden hummed the tune to one of the songs as they walked out into the mellow late-May evening. Happy chatter surrounded them as others left the theater. Jazz drifted along the wind from down the street. Somewhere up the river, a boat blew its horn. And Katie was snuggled close to his side. It was the perfect evening.

"What are you humming?" Her voice teased a grin out of him.

"I was just thinking how convenient it was that your name fit in this song." He winked at her before singing the words out loud. "Ka-therine. Lady librar-ian."

"Ugh." She shook her head. "How did you find out my name is Katherine?"

"Lucky guess." He grabbed her hand and spun her around as they stopped to wait for a light to change. "Why? What's wrong with it?"

"Katherine is just so … it's an old lady name." She rubbed a hand across her face.

"I think it's lovely."

"You're crazy."

"Crazy for you." He pointed to the parking garage. "Shall we?"

"Camden." She stopped and looked down the street. "We're pretty close to the river, right?"

"Just a few blocks away." What was she thinking about?

"Do you think there's somewhere down there we could sit for a bit?" She played with the edge of her purse strap. "But you probably need to get back. I mean, it's not exactly early and we live clear on the other side …"

"Come on." He took her hand and started leading her west. "There's a park somewhere not too far from here. Let's see if we can find it."

Would she open up to him? Explain some things? Make sense of what Jodie had been trying to tell him that last day in Georgia? Something told him if she could shed light on all that, it could be the turning point in their relationship. Otherwise, they probably had no real chance at making this work.

She was silent until he settled them on a bench overlooking Ol' Man River. A barge pushed through the brown waters, heading toward New Orleans. The lights on the bridges cast a romantic glow on the scene, though he had a feeling this conversation wouldn't be romantic … at least not at first.

Would she ever speak? She sat still as a statue, stiff under the arm he'd wrapped about her shoulders. Her gaze remained fixed straight ahead, her breath more shallow than normal.

"I supposed you're wondering about me. About why I can't handle …" She broke off and smoothed down her skirt.

"You don't have to tell me anything you don't want to." He

tucked a soft curl behind her ear. "I'm here if you want to talk. And I'm going to be here even if you don't."

"My family used to drive around and look at Christmas lights each year."

The change in subject made him frown. What? But something inside prompted him to be still and just listen.

"Ten years ago. Well, it'll be eleven this year, we were loading up to go. Jodie and I argued about who got to sit where. She usually sat behind the driver's seat, and I usually sat on the other side. But that year she'd convinced me her seat had the better lights, so I was adamant that was where I wanted to sit. I ended up winning, and we set off, mugs of hot chocolate in hand, music playing on the radio."

She took a deep breath. "About half an hour into the drive, we were passing a particularly extravagant home. It was one of those with lights synchronized to the music, and it danced during the performance. Dad had slowed down so we could watch as we passed. Next thing I know—"

He pulled her to his chest as a sob erupted from her. "Shh. It's okay. You don't have to."

"No. I need to tell you. Maybe it will help you understand." She pushed back. "The lights had distracted someone else too. Someone who'd had too many drinks earlier that evening at a company Christmas party. Dad swerved to avoid being hit, but the drunk still crashed into the passenger side of our car."

Katie swiped at her eyes, swallowed. "I woke up to find the other driver standing over me, tugging at my seat belt. His breath reeked of alcohol. Jodie was passed out beside me. Mom and Dad were unconscious in the front. I think maybe he thought I was the only one alive."

He rubbed his hands up and down her arms, wishing he could offer more comfort than that simple gesture. Nothing seemed enough.

"He got me out, laid me on the ground. Tried to do CPR, I think, even though I was conscious and fighting him." Her lips pinched together until they were white before she relaxed again.

"The EMTs finally arrived and pulled him away from me. I had bruises on my arms for several weeks from his hands. Jodie—we thought we'd lost her for a while. Then we found out she'd live but ... never walk again. The impact had broken her back and severed her spinal cord. Mom and Dad came out with some bruises and concussions, but nothing worse."

"Jodie seems to be doing well." He inwardly berated himself for staring at Jodie's wheelchair when they were in Georgia. That had probably only made things harder for Katie.

"She's doing great. She told me when we were down there that it wasn't my fault she ended up that way."

"Of course it wasn't your fault!" He leaned over to look into her eyes. "Why would you think it was?"

"Because that was my seat!" Katie slammed her fists onto her lap. "It should have been me with the broken back, not her. She can't even get in the floor and play with her little boy."

"But she can still do so much else. And I'm sure she wouldn't want you to have a broken back either." Camden clasped her face in his hands.

Katie shook her head as much as she could with him holding it. "No. But she said she'd tricked me because she wanted that seat more anyway. She said it had more leg room."

"You know it's not her fault either?" Camden wasn't prepared for this. He didn't know the right words to say. *God, please help me know when to speak and when to be silent. Give me what she needs so I can help her through this.*

"Jodie said it wasn't either of our faults. That it was the fault of the drunk driver." Her tears trickled down the sides of his thumbs resting on her cheeks. "He's the reason I can't handle being around the smell of alcohol. It takes me right back to that night, the fear, the anger, the terror as he pulled on my arms, pressed his mouth to mine ...”

Camden couldn't stand it anymore and pulled her to him, cradling her against his chest. “I'm so sorry I couldn't protect you from that. And that I didn't protect you more on our trip.”

She tried to protest.

But he shushed her. “If I'd known you were battling PTSD, I would've made sure to whisk you away to do something else. Why did Bree think you could handle it?”

“She didn't realize it was that bad until we were down there.” Katie leaned back and wiped her cheeks. “Remember at the ballgame when she tried to get me to leave early? That's because she saw how bad it got earlier that week. But I was too stubborn. And I didn't want to give up any of those minutes I had with you. I was afraid it would be the last time we'd be together.”

“I told you we'd find a way to see each other again.” He grinned at her.

“Yes, but none of it seemed real then. I mean, a girl doesn't normally get to bring a boyfriend back as a souvenir from her vacation, you know.” A tremulous smile graced her lips. “I didn't think I was going to get to keep you.”

Camden laughed. “I'd love to be your souvenir. Does that mean I need to come live on a shelf in your apartment?”

“No!” She swatted him. “But maybe ...”

“Maybe what?”

“Bree wants us to bring a date to her wedding. But it's not proper for a girl to ask a guy on a date, is it? Are you one of those old-fashioned guys who always has to do the asking?”

“You could try it and see.” He lifted an eyebrow.

She opened her mouth, closed it again, then tried once more. “Camden, would you please escort me to Bree's wedding in a few weeks? I'm likely to be very emotional and crazy, though. Consider yourself warned."

Laughing, he pressed a quick kiss to her lips. "I'd love to. Haven't you figured out yet that I don't mind your emotional craziness? I grew up with two sisters, remember?"

She shook her head. "And I'm not any worse than them, huh?"

"Much nicer. They always picked on me." He wrinkled his nose.

"Ha!"

"You don't believe me?" He clasped his hands to his chest.

"I have a big sister, too, remember?" She grinned. "I believe you."

He rose and offered her his hand, and they walked back to the car. It was late, and even though he'd assured her the streets downtown were safe, he didn't want to risk it any further. He snuggled her into his side as they meandered down the sidewalk.

"Will you do me a favor?" He held her car door open for her and let her slide in.

"What's that?" She studied him as he sat on the other side and started the engine.

"I have a friend, someone from church actually. He's a counselor." He tapped the steering wheel while he waited for another car to pass so he could back out.

"Oh." It was as if a veil had fallen across her face.

"Hear me out. I've actually had some sessions with him in the past, and he's really easy to talk to. I think it might help if you could talk to a professional. He might have some suggestions for ways to combat the panic attacks besides simply avoiding the triggers. Not that we can't do that, but I'd love for you to be able to go to more ballgames in the future without having to deal with the anxiety."

"You?" She shook her head. "That's a lot to process. You had to talk to a counselor? And you want to take me to ballgames in the future?"

"I'd love to do things with you as long as you'll let me. I know it's early in our relationship, but I could see this going on for years. And yes, I'm not perfect either. Remember how I told you that my fiancée left me several years ago?" And amazingly enough, saying that didn't hurt anymore.

"I'm sorry." Her hand covered his, and he wove their fingers together. "I guess I was so focused on myself that I didn't even consider the fact that other people needed to talk to counselors. Plus, I guess it was a little annoying to have someone else tell me I should go talk to someone like that."

"Someone else?"

"Jodie suggested the same thing." Katie stared out the window as they passed the southern half of Memphis. "I don't think she realized how much I was still haunted by all of it until she and I talked."

"Oh, man. To be lumped with an older sister in the advice-giving department ..." He made a face.

"Ha, ha. You know what I mean." She leaned her head on his shoulder. "You really think there's a chance for us?"

"I'm praying for it every day." He whispered the words around a lump in his throat.

"Me too."

# 20

S tanding in front of Katie's door, Camden rang the bell. *Finally.* After two weeks, she'd agreed to go see his counselor friend Paul. He'd sweetened the deal by offering to take her out for dinner afterward.

Rustling sounded inside the apartment along with a few giggles. His heart picked up speed as he braced himself to see her again. Just the thought set his heart skipping.

Katie's white floral sundress fluttered as a breeze stirred up the same moment she opened the door. Bree lifted a hand in greeting from behind her.

"Hi."

Camden gave them both a big grin. "Good afternoon, ladies."

"As of today, less than a month until I'm Mrs. Bree Hart." Bree squealed and beamed him a smile bigger than any he'd seen before.

"Not that you're counting or anything." Katie rolled her eyes but smiled too.

"I can't wait until y'all are engaged and I can remind you of this conversation." Bree pointed her finger back and forth between Katie and Camden.

He lifted a brow and wrapped an arm around Katie. "Engaged, huh? After only two real dates? Katie been telling you things she hasn't let me in on yet?"

"Let's not rush things. Too much." Katie's finger poked his side, and he jerked away. "One wedding at a time."

"Okay, but after my wedding, I'll have plenty of time to help plan yours." Bree winked, her laugh echoing off the concrete balcony where they stood.

"And why are you so certain I'm going to be needing to plan a wedding?" Katie crossed her arms over her chest.

"Let's just say something tells me when I toss my bouquet, God's going to make sure it lands in the right hands." Bree wagged her eyebrows.

Camden couldn't help but send up another prayer of thanks that he'd run into these two on vacation three weeks ago. Despite their picking, their friendship ran deep. And he was honored to have that friendship extended his way now.

"And since I'm her date, I'll get a front row seat to see that."

"Camden!" Katie sent a half-hearted scowl his way. "You're supposed to be on my side."

"You're her date!" Bree threw her arms around him and gave a tiny squeal. "She didn't tell me she'd asked you."

Katie stiffened at his side, and Camden looked her way, hoping she wasn't fighting jealousy over her friend's exuberant display of affection. But Katie's focus was on the parking lot, not on him. Camden followed her line of sight and saw a guy standing there, ramrod straight and with a sour expression on his face.

"Bree." Katie caught Bree right as she was about to say something else.

Bree turned and froze, too, before a laugh of either shock or chagrin escaped her. "Nathan!"

She was out the door, down the stairs, and throwing her arms around him in less time than it took for Camden to process that this was the elusive fiancé he'd heard so much about. But for someone weeks away from his wedding, Nathan Hart didn't look happy to see his betrothed. In fact, if Camden had to define the vibes coming off Nathan's body language, he'd say they ran more along the lines of livid wrath.

"I had no idea he was coming today. I guess maybe Bree didn't either." Katie pitched her voice low, but her eyes never strayed from the direction of her friends. "They've been having some disagreements lately, but I thought maybe things were better after they talked last night. The way she acted this morning made it seem all was good again. But his face doesn't fit that, does it?"

Camden slid his arm over Katie's shoulders. "Maybe it was a misunderstanding. With them apart for the last few weeks, there had to be some miscommunication, right?"

"Right." But Katie's voice didn't hold much belief in its tone.

Bree stepped back when Nathan didn't return her hug. He still stood stiffly, as though made of stone. The alarm on Camden's phone reminded him they needed to leave if they were to make the appointment on time. But something told him Katie wasn't about to abandon her friend when the situation looked so stormy.

Bree's hands flew around as she evidently explained something. With a shake of his head, Nathan turned aside and seemed to struggle with himself several moments before turning back. Though it still looked taut, Nathan's mouth moved in response. Bree's shoulders slumped.

"Do you think we should offer to help?" Katie's whisper held a note of tears.

"I'm not sure we'd do any good. Something tells me I might be part of the problem." Camden resisted the urge to pull Katie from the turbulent scene. Much as he agreed with her desire to ease the tension, the way Nathan looked, he probably wouldn't welcome people he considered to be meddling.

"What do you mean, you're part of the problem?"

"Bree was hugging me when he walked up, right?" Camden glanced down at Katie. "Do you think Nathan jumped to the wrong conclusion?"

"Oh, no." Katie covered her mouth. "He was pretty upset about you guys joining us on our trip. But Bree explained you weren't interested in her. And she had no interest in you—no offense."

"None taken. Was he jealous?"

"We thought maybe since he'd been part of our group of friends for years, he was just upset he'd never been invited on one of our trips, but two strangers got to join us." Katie frowned and glanced her friends' way again. "Are you thinking he thought Bree was cheating?"

Camden tugged Katie tighter to his side, hoping he was wrong. Because that's exactly what he thought. And the way Nathan now cut his hands through the air and shook his finger between Bree and where Camden stood, he wondered if maybe he should say something.

---

This was ridiculous. Katie understood Camden's caution against intervening, but Nathan and Bree loved each other—were perfect for each other. They shouldn't be fighting. Especially not this close to their happily ever after.

She took a step away from the comfort of Camden's embrace and toward the stairs just as Nathan reached out and grabbed Bree's left hand. With a couple tugs, the diamond she'd been so proud of slipped off and was tucked away in Nathan's shirt pocket. He turned on his toes and marched off into the parking lot while Bree slid down into a puddle where he'd left her.

Katie shoved Camden aside and rushed to Bree, wrapping her up in her arms. The sunshine on their backs now felt cruel and menacing instead of the happy, warm embrace she'd considered it earlier. Bree's sobs shook her whole body, though no sound came out except for an occasional sniffle.

There was no point in asking questions. Not until this maelstrom passed. So, Katie held her friend and rubbed circles on her back. She didn't even realize Camden had joined her until he pressed some tissues in her hand.

"Thanks." She mouthed the words, appreciating how he slid down on the curb nearby instead of trying to help in any other way. He was there if she needed him. Either that or he didn't know what to do. Although he'd said tears didn't scare him because of his sisters.

Regardless, now was not the time or place to try and figure out her new boyfriend. Bree needed her, and she'd be here as long as it took. Even if they got stepped on by people coming and going from their own apartments.

Bree let out an extra-long shudder and shook her head. "Did that really happen?"

Katie helped her stand and guided her over to the curb, where Camden scooted to make room. "You tell us. We aren't certain of exact details."

"Nathan." The name came out more moan—an epitome of anguish—than simply a statement.

"We saw him."

"He said I'd been cheating. That he'd had enough cheating in his life. Couldn't stand to marry a girl who couldn't even stay true to him ... until the wedding." Bree buried her head on Katie's shoulder and sobbed again.

"This is because he saw you hugging Camden?"

Bree's answer came out muffled. "I ... don't ... know."

"But Bree, didn't you tell him why you'd hugged him? Or remind him you hug everyone whether they want it or not?" Katie had been the recipient of several of those embraces.

"He wouldn't listen." Bree sat up and mopped at her face with an already moisture-laden tissue. "Just said the same things over and over again."

"Why did he come? Were you expecting him?"

Bree shook her head. "I had no idea. We talked last night, and he didn't say anything about surprising me this afternoon. In fact, I thought I'd finally gotten it through his head that I felt nothing for Camden or Ryan."

"Maybe we can call him and help explain after he has time to cool off." Camden's hand rested on Katie's shoulders, and she was never more grateful for the comfort of his touch.

"I doubt he'd listen." Bree ran her fingertips over the spot where his diamond had rested for a year. "He said he never wanted to see me again."

Camden's phone dinged—probably reminding him they were supposed to be heading to see his friend. A few people clomped down the stairs, shooting strange glances Bree's way as they walked past. Katie glanced over at Camden, but he didn't appear to have any more idea what to do than she did.

"How about let's go in and splash some water on your face now?" Katie gave Bree's fingers a tug.

"I'm keeping you guys from your appointment." Bree hiccuped as she stood. "And your date."

"So, we'll reschedule." Katie shot Camden a look and

though he'd opened his mouth, he closed it. Right now, Bree's problems were more urgent than hers.

"But Katie, you've been fighting your battle for so long. You should go." Bree slumped onto the sofa. "Besides, maybe things will make sense if I can just think them through alone."

"We're already too late to make the counseling appointment today." Katie grabbed a washcloth from the bathroom and ran warm water over it. "So, there's no point in discussing that any further."

"But you were going on a date, too, right? There's no point in me ruining your whole evening."

"Bree, being here for you is not ruining my evening." Katie knelt beside her friend. She'd make it up to Camden later, but if he really loved her the way he said he did, he'd understand.

"What if we just go pick up something to eat and bring it back here?" Camden's question ruined her hopes of him understanding.

"I'm not sure I could eat." Bree pressed the cloth to her eyes. "But please don't starve yourselves on my account. You should go."

"But—"

"Katie." Camden motioned with his head for her to come in the other room.

"I'll be right back." She squeezed Bree's arm and followed him into the kitchen.

Camden glanced over her shoulder. "Bree seems to want to be alone for a while. Let's give her some time to come to grips with it. Go grab some dinner and then come back. Maybe she'll be more ready to talk then."

She wanted to argue, but knew he was right. "Fine."

"We're going out for just a while, Bree. Want us to bring something back?" Camden spun his keys around his finger.

"Seriously not hungry guys."

"We'll bring something anyway." Katie wrapped her arms around Bree again. "You might change your mind by the time we get back."

Bree gave a quick nod. "Thanks, Katie."

It took everything in Katie to walk out her door. Not like she was going to be good company for her boyfriend, for worrying about her friend.

What could've gone wrong? Was it really all about Camden and his cousin? A big lump of yucky settled in her gut. If so, then it was her fault too.

"What's wrong?" Camden nudged her as they made their way down to his car. "Besides the obvious, there's something else eating at you. It was like a veil of blue slipped over your shoulders just now."

"It's my fault."

Camden froze and turned her to face him. "No."

"Yes. They encouraged you guys to keep coming on our trip because they wanted us to get together. I was selfish. If I'd just exchanged numbers with you and promised to reach out after the trip none of this would've happened."

"You don't know but something else might've broken them up instead. It looked like he was almost looking for an excuse to call things off."

"What?" Katie blinked. "But why?"

"I don't know. But something tells me there's more to this story than we know. It almost looked to me like he arrived with a chip on his shoulder easy enough for a butterfly to knock off." Camden shook his head. "I just have this hunch there's some background we're missing."

Traffic was slow as they headed toward what Camden described as his favorite chicken place.

"And you taking on the blame for this just confirms we

need to reschedule your counseling session too." Camden hit the blinker.

"I'm glad I could prove my brokenness even more."

"That's not what I meant, and you know it."

"Do I?" Katie fiddled with the edge of her seat belt. "Because it seems like since our first date, all you've done is pressure me to see this Paul guy."

"Because I want to help you." He banged his hands against the steering wheel.

"Maybe you should've just left me with Bree tonight. Maybe this a sign."

Throwing the car in park, he jerked the key to shut the ignition off. "A sign of what?"

"Nathan and Bree were perfect for each other. We haven't known each other even a month yet. They were together over three years!"

"What does their relationship have to do with ours?"

Katie turned to him, fighting back the tears pooling in her eyes. "Don't you see? If a couple so obviously meant to be can't have their happily ever after, what chance do we have? A broken girl and a guy who wants to fix her. That's not a good start for any relationship."

"You're going to let Nathan and Bree's fight drive us to have one of our own?" Camden's jaw shifted, as if he bit back more words.

Katie shook her head. "Can you just take me home, Camden? I can't talk about this right now."

"When can you talk about it?"

"I don't know."

Ten minutes later, he pulled back into the parking lot. "I'm not giving up on us yet."

Katie didn't reply. Instead, she reached for the door handle and tugged, but it wouldn't open.

"I'll unlock it in a minute, but I want you to listen."

Narrowing her eyes, she turned back just enough to see the pain on his face that echoed the anguish vibrating through her own chest.

"Do not let Nathan's jealousy lead you to regret the closeness growing between us. Because I can't regret it."

"I don't regret you." Katie fought back more tears. "Just that it led to Bree's heartbreak."

"So, we think and brainstorm. Maybe we can come up with a way to get them back together."

"It might take a miracle."

"We happen to know Someone who specializes in those." Camden pointed toward the sky. "Pray. Be there for Bree. And let's both see what we can come up with to help her find a way back to her happily ever after."

She shook her head. "I don't know ..."

"If you're saying our happily ever after won't happen unless theirs does, I'm definitely going to do everything I can to make it happen." Camden hit the button to unlock the doors.

Katie burst from the vehicle and up the stairs. Bree had disappeared into her room and sobs echoed through the otherwise quiet apartment. How could Katie undo the pain of today? How could this be fixed?

# 21

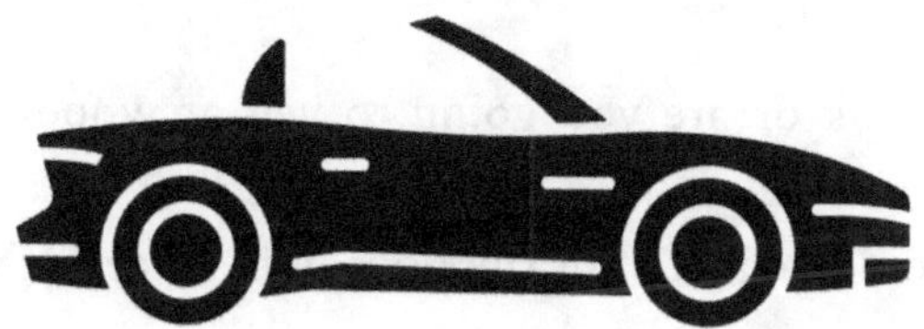

"Oh, hi." Katie stood frozen in the doorway the next Saturday.

"Hi to you too." Of course it was Camden who had knocked. Who else would it be?

Nathan had yet to relent in the fight with Bree. Hadn't even taken any of her phone calls this week. So, Katie and Bree had started the mad scramble to cancel all the intricate plans of Bree's wedding.

Which was why Bree had driven home to Kentucky this weekend. And Katie was at the apartment by herself and actually talking to Skye on the phone. The flighty friend had been as comforting as possible from miles away.

"Who is it, Katie?" Skye's voice pulled her out of her frozen mode.

"It's Camden." If Katie's voice tripped a bit over his name, it was only due to the dust in the air. Not from the fact she'd missed him like crazy this week. It couldn't be that.

"Oh, I can let you go—"

"No!" Katie needed the support of someone even if Skye

wasn't in the room. "No, it's okay. I'm not even sure why he's here."

"And wouldn't it be easier to find out if you talked to him?" Since when was Skye one to give advice?

Camden rubbed the back of his neck. "Can I come in for a minute?"

Katie shifted her weight from foot to foot and then stepped back.

"Can I talk or are you going to yell at whoever's on the phone again?"

She should've just shut the door in his face. "It's just Skye. Talk."

A squeak of protest rang in her ear.

One of his brows lifted higher than the other, but he nodded. "I got you another appointment."

"I can't go yet. I can't focus on my problems when Bree's seem so much bigger right now. Maybe after we get her situation all cleaned up, I'll try again."

"Katie!"

Both of them said it at the same time. How could they possibly be ganging up on her when they weren't even in the same state?

"Should I just put this on speaker?" Katie held the phone away from her head.

"If it will help you listen, go ahead." Camden motioned toward the button.

Katie blinked, but then turned it on. "Skye, you're on speaker. Apparently, whatever Camden came to say can be said in front of you too."

"Sweet. First row to a showdown. Just what I wanted this afternoon."

"Look." Camden shoved his hands in his pockets and shifted his weight. "I didn't come to fight. I didn't want to fight last week, either. But what you said last Saturday, when you pointed out if Bree and Nathan couldn't have their happily ever after, what shot did we have? Well, I disagree."

She narrowed her eyes, but didn't say anything.

"Why should our relationship rely on theirs? That doesn't even make sense. Every couple has to figure out their own relationship, and if we go around comparing ourselves to others—who are also made up of imperfect people, by the way—we won't have any time to focus on strengthening our own."

As much as she wanted to protest, she couldn't. He was right, whether she was ready to admit it or not.

"I'm more than willing to help you get Bree and Nathan back together, but I don't want to sit and wait for that to happen before we do something to fix the mess we've made of our own romance. Katie, I missed you like crazy this week. I know we're just getting started, and probably have lots of fights ahead of us, but can't we make up?"

"Awww," Skye shouted through the phone. "Cam, my offer from a few weeks ago still stands. If Katie doesn't want you, come find me."

"I'm about to hang up on you, Skye." Katie tried to keep her voice stern, but her lips kept twitching up in to a smile. A giggle escaped.

"Can you guys just make up already so we can get back to what we were discussing before?" Skye huffed before laughing too.

Camden took a step closer, reached out and cupped her shoulder. "Please?"

Katie pressed her lips together, took a deep breath, and then nodded. "I missed you too."

The next thing she knew, she was crushed in a hug, her ear pressed to his heartbeat, and her arms wrapped around his waist. And it felt like a piece of her that had been missing all week slipped back into place. He leaned back just far enough to press a quick kiss to her lips.

"Now, wrap up your talk with Skye. Your appointment is in an hour and a half."

Katie swatted his shoulder. "You showed up here expecting me to just go?"

"Nope. I gave myself almost two hours to talk you into it." He winked and she couldn't help but join in Skye's guffaws.

"We were actually brainstorming. Trying to find ways to get Nathan and Bree to talk to each other." She tugged Camden to the couch and curled up next to him. "He won't take her calls or anything. But she's too stubborn to drive to Nashville and corner him."

"So, we need a way to get them together but where they won't expect that's what we're up to." Camden wrapped his arm around her shoulders and tugged her closer.

"Right." Skye chimed in. "Any ideas?"

Camden chuckled. "I don't suppose we could send them on a road trip? That seemed to work for Katie and me."

"Seriously, Camden?" Katie shook her head.

"No. That might actually work. But not a road trip." Skye tapped something on her end. "And I actually know someone who can probably help us. Did we ever find out what Nathan had booked for their honeymoon?"

"Nooo." Katie frowned. "But they sort of need to get married before they can go on a honeymoon, Skye."

"Or do they?" Camden leaned closer to the phone. "Are we actually thinking along the same lines?"

"What are you guys talking about?" Katie glanced between the man beside her and the device in her hand.

"Depending on what Nathan booked, it's probably nonrefundable if he hasn't already canceled it. They only give you so many days to get your money back." Skye hummed a minute.

"Which means, that trip is just sitting there waiting to be taken."

Camden snapped. "So, we just need to convince both of them to go without the other one knowing."

Katie's eyes widened. "How do we do that?"

Skye chimed in again. "I happen to have access to Nathan's brother, Josh. He's interning up here for the first month of the summer. And I bet he'd be willing to help. Let me work on it on this end, and I'll get back to you."

"Skye, are you sure this is a good idea?" Katie's question came too late.

The phone call had ended.

"I'm not sure about this. What if they end up staying in the same room or something? They're not married yet. What if it were us? Would you want someone to do that to us?"

"I can think of something I'd like us to do right now." Camden's voice was low.

She looked up to find him studying her. "What?"

"This." He pressed his lips to hers.

"Camden, seriously."

"I haven't seen you except at a distance for a week now. Gotta make up for lost time."

She giggled and pushed away. "If you want me to go to a counseling appointment in a few minutes, I need to go change out of these sweatpants."

"Fine." He rolled his eyes but then grinned and released her.

Before closing her door, she leaned back out. "You really think we have a chance?"

"So long as we don't base our relationship on anyone else's. The only ones allowed to dictate our love are you, me, and God." He pointed up.

"Okay." And she floated into her room to change.

"Are you sure this is going to work?" A few days later, Katie checked the clock again, hoping Bree came home from the grocery store quickly.

"It has to." Skye's eye roll was exaggerated on the screen of Katie's tablet. "As much as you both drove me crazy with all the wedding talk, I have to admit Nathan and Bree are perfect for each other. So, we trap them on a ship for a week and they should remember that, too, right?"

"For someone so averse to falling in love, you sure are eager to help other people do it." Katie pushed one of her curls back from her face.

"It's a style that looks much better on others than it does on me." Skye winked.

"Just you wait. Someday I bet you're going to want to try it on for size."

"Not anytime in the near future." Skye shook her head. "My father's threatening to take my keys if I can't find a job soon."

"Well, you are a college graduate now."

"That doesn't mean I know what I want to be." A slight whine tinged Skye's voice. "I'm scrambling to come up with a plan to buy myself some more time. I can't lose my convertible!"

"You could ... get a job." Katie raised her eyebrows and shot Skye what she hoped was a mom look.

"Ugh. Be serious."

The door opened, and Bree pushed through, plastic bags draped over both arms. "A little help here?"

"Hang on, Skye." Katie jumped up and grabbed the gallon of milk from under her roommate's arm, as well as a few of the bags that looked most likely to be dropped.

"Did you just call me Skye?" Bree huffed as she set the groceries on the counter.

"No. I was video chatting with her in the living room." Katie glanced through the bags, set the ice cream in the freezer, and waved at the rest. "This can wait. Come say hi to Skye."

"It won't take me very long to put these away, and then I will." Bree pulled several cans out to prove her point.

Katie linked their arms together and tugged. "She wanted to see you. She has an idea."

"An idea?" Bree resisted, but Katie was stronger.

"Bree?" Skye's voice called through the device.

"Hey, Skye." Bree sank onto the couch and picked up the tablet.

"How are you?"

Katie sat beside her roommate and resisted rolling her own eyes at the inane question.

"How do you think I am?" Bree's voice held a hint of tears. "I've spent the last two weeks either trying to get ahold of Nathan or canceling wedding plans."

"I'm sorry." Skye's nose scrunched up. "It sounds like you need a vacation."

"Pretty sure vacation's what got me into this mess in the first place." The bitterness in Bree's words pricked Katie's chest.

"Well ... I happened to run into Josh the other day—"

"Wait." Bree held the screen up higher. "Josh? Josh Hart?"

"Yeah. He's interning at my home congregation for part of this summer. Didn't you know?"

"I'd forgotten."

Skye waved her hands. "Anyway, he was with Nathan last week, and Nathan was griping about how he couldn't get a refund on the honeymoon trip because of the company he'd booked it through. Something about refunds only given in cases of natural disaster or something like that."

Bree's eyes narrowed. "So, he's going on our honeymoon? Without me?"

"Nope. He doesn't want to travel. So that trip's going to waste."

Bree glanced at Katie and then back at Skye. "That doesn't sound like Nathan. He hates wasting money."

Her face only slightly mischievous, Skye shrugged. "Josh's words. I'm simply passing them on. But it gave me an idea."

"I'm not even sure I want to know." Bree leaned back against the cushions.

Katie nudged Bree with her shoulder. "Hear her out. I think it's a good idea too."

"She got you involved in this ridiculousness?" Bree raised an eyebrow. "Skye, I don't feel like going and doing New York by myself. With no one to kiss on top of the Empire State Building, what's the point?"

A laugh burst from Skye. "Here's the kicker. He didn't book a trip to New York. He booked a cruise. How does a week of sunshine and sea sound?"

"A cruise!" Bree punched the couch cushion. "No wonder he wouldn't give me any confirmation on what all we'd be doing. I would've packed all wrong for that. What was he thinking?"

Skye shrugged. "I don't know. But Josh said he could get all the information from Nathan if you want to go. He feels rather bad about how his brother has been acting, though he didn't shed any new insights on the reasoning. But I think you should take the trip. It's only fair after having to go through the stress of canceling everything—and maybe it will make up for a few of those down payments you couldn't get refunded. Serves Nathan right not to get his money back too."

"That's rather tacky of you." Bree sighed. "A honeymoon without a groom? Doesn't sound like much fun, does it?"

"It could be. You can come back with a nice tan—maybe even find a guy to fall in love with like Katie."

"Too soon, Skye!" Katie protested before Bree did.

"Besides, there can't be two guys out there perfect for me." Bree shook her head. "Although the thought of a week of sun and surf does sound nice. And it's not like I'm doing anything else right now. No nibbles on the job search since I had to change the area I was looking."

"Perfect. I'll get everything from Josh and get it to you ASAP. I almost wish I were joining you."

"You really want to risk losing your car for a cruise?" Katie shot a look through the internet to remind Skye that no one else *could* go with Bree since they had Josh working on a plan for the other ticket.

"No." Skye made a face. "And my father said he's serious this time."

Bree let out something between and a snort and a sigh. "You and that car."

"Yeah, well, to each her own and all that."

Camden pulled Katie closer to him on the swing he'd recently installed on his back porch. "Bree get off okay?"

"Seemed to. She texted that she made her flight on time and would let me know before the ship left dock." Katie huffed. "I wonder if she'll keep that promise when she finds out who else is going on this trip too."

"I still can't believe our plan worked."

"It definitely took all of us to pull it off."

"Think they'll feel set up?"

"If we ever had a fight that bad—and I'm not saying we will, but it might happen—I'd hope my friends would try everything in the world to get us back together."

"Oh, yeah?" The feeling of forever settled in his middle, and he was the most comfortable he'd ever been. Even more so than when he'd been engaged to Jen several years before.

"That sounds crazy, though, right?"

"Nope." He rested his head against her curls. "Not crazy at all."

"They're just so perfect for each other. Her *joi de vivre* and his down-to-earthness meshed so well." Her sigh was bone deep. "It didn't show at all in the one time you got to see him, but we're hoping with them trapped on a ship for a week with nowhere to really hide from each other, maybe they'll be able to find the love that was there before our trip in May. I want my friend back where she doesn't seem more zombie than human being."

"Well, then I hope the plan works." He moved the swing in an easy rhythm as the crickets chirped all around them. "Skye and Bree were able to pull off their matchmaking schemes when it came to you and me. Maybe Skye and you will do just as well."

"I still can't believe you hung my mask in your front hall-way." Katie craned her head around to look up at him.

"I liked it."

"I hated it at the time."

Camden remembered. That day in New Orleans had been full of highs and lows. But it had also taught him a lot about the girl now in his arms.

"Just think of it as a beacon of hope. You had no idea when we spent that day together, we'd end up here, like this. And Bree and Nathan probably won't start their trip off on good terms, either, considering they haven't spoken since he called off the wedding."

"The wedding that was supposed to be yesterday." Katie reached over and wove her fingers through his. "What am I supposed to do with that dress? It couldn't be returned because it had been altered to fit only me."

"Save it. If they get back together, I'm sure you'll still be a bridesmaid—"

"Assuming she forgives me for setting her up on this trip."

"She will if they're together again." He gave her a squeeze. "And then you'll need that dress."

They were quiet for a few moments, simply enjoying the calm of the evening before the start of another busy week.

"Is it still okay for me to pick you up for counseling this week?" Camden didn't look her way, afraid she might refuse.

"If you really want to. Isn't it boring sitting in the lobby while I'm in the session, though?"

Relief swept over him that she wasn't against going back. "I don't mind. It's sort of nice having an hour to do nothing. And I get to see you before and after. Do you think it's helping?"

"I mean, I've only had one session so far." When her shoulder shrugged, it dug into his side, but he didn't mind. "But I think it will help. And after everything we've just done to Bree and Nathan, I might need to work through the angst that caused too. She might even want to join me when they get back, if this plan falls through."

"Our plan has to work." Camden's lips twitched.

"Oh? Why's that?" Katie straightened and raised an eyebrow.

"I need you to catch that bouquet."

She gave him a little shove, but he caught her hands and pulled her in for a kiss.

"Who knew I'd be bringing a boyfriend home as a souvenir? I hope Bree gets to too."

"Then only Skye will be left."

"And she's in Colorado."

"I thought she had to get a job to keep her car?"

Katie nodded, her hair tickling his chin. "Something about working for her sister this summer to buy some time."

"Well, surely there are souvenir boyfriends in Colorado." Camden chuckled.

"Don't tell Skye. She doesn't think she's ready for anything to do with being an adult."

"She just hasn't found the right souvenir yet." He whispered the words right in Katie's ear.

"And you have?" Her hazel eyes blinked as she tilted her face up to him.

"I hope to hold on to this one for a long time."

"Me too."

# AUTHOR'S NOTE

Hello, dear reader.

I have to be honest. I am not one to believe in love at first sight, or even the concept of falling in love. I consider love to be more of an action we choose to give. That being said, I do believe love can grow from an early attraction.

When I first had the idea for this story, I wasn't sure where it was going to go. I simply knew the three girls were going to be on a roadtrip together, and the boys were going to tag along. The biggest hurdle would be building a romance between two of the characters that was strong enough to be believable in such a short time. I hope I did it justice.

As to the locations? I've been to three of them. For Gulf Shores, I did a lot of research and used my experience visiting other areas of the gulf coast for those scenes. And, I have to admit I had a ton of fun revisiting these places in my memories, despite not having had the chance to physically be in most of the areas in years and years. I hope you enjoyed the ride, too.

If you enjoyed this story, I'd love for you to share it with a friend. Also, if you can, please leave a review. Reviews, even short ones, help authors by not only lifting our spirits but also letting others know that people think our story is worth reading. I appreciate it so much.

Be sure to look for Bree's and Skye's stories coming in December 2022 and June 2023. I'm sure you'll want to know about their own roadtrips.

If you'd like to keep up with me, feel free to check out my website at http://abitofanguish.weebly.com or facebook.com/amyanguishauthor.

God bless you!

Amy

# DISCUSSION QUESTIONS

1.  Katie is afraid to pursue anything romantic with Camden because she doesn't think they'll ever see each other again. Do you think a relationship has a chance when founded on something so temporary?

2.  Each of the girls on the trip isn't completely honest with the others, hiding how much they dread no longer having their relationship after college. Do you have friends you were close to in school with whom you found a way to remain close afterwards? Have you ever let something eat you up inside to the point that it caused strife in the relationships around you?

3.  Camden isn't sure about a new relationship considering the way the last one ended. Is it easy to overcome the fear of history repeating itself?

4.  Katie tends to be introverted and quieter than her friends, nervous when placed in new situations. The girls' differences

not only make their friendship stronger, but also tend to help them through the different scenarios on their trips. Do you have friends who balance you out and make life better despite being completely different from you?

5. The girls covered a lot of miles on this trip, as they tried to fill it up with lots of fun. If you could go on a roadtrip with friends, would you rather hit lots of different spots or stay in one place and get to do more there? Any of the places the girls traveled now on your wish list?

6. Katie allowed her old insecurities and fears to fester and become a sort of PTSD in her life, triggering anxiety attacks and hindering her from being able to live life as fully as she wanted. It's so easy to keep worries and guilt inside instead of allowing others to help, but it's not the best choice. Have you ever allowed something to eat you up for too long so that it started to affect parts of your life?

7. Katie and Skye disagreed about the best way to see a town. Katie wanted to explore the history and culture, while Skye was all about the fun. Which way do you tend to lean on your vacations? Do you try to find a balance?

8. Katie and Camden both share a love for the smell of books when they first enter the library. What's your favorite part of a library? The smell, the quiet atmosphere, the possibilities?

9. Think back to one of your favorite trips. What moments or events stand out in a positive way, the ones that went according to plan or the ones that took your trip in an unexpected direction?

10.  We get to read more about the girls in future books. What are you hoping happens to each of them? Do you find yourself more curious about the next part of Skye's story or Bree's?

# ABOUT THE AUTHOR

Amy R Anguish grew up a preacher's kid, and in spite of having lived in seven different states that are all south of the Mason Dixon line, she is not a football fan. Currently, she resides in Tennessee with her husband, daughter, and son, and usually a bossy cat or two. Amy has an English degree from Freed-Hardeman University that she intends to use to glorify God, and she wants her stories to show that while Christians face real struggles, it can still work out for good.

*No Place Like Home*

**Can love secure Adrian's wandering heart?**

Roots are overrated, at least to someone like Adrian Stewart, preacher's kid, who has never lived anywhere longer than six years. That's why her job with MidUSLogIn Inc., is so perfect for her—lots of travel, and staying nowhere long enough to have it feel like home. But when work takes her to Memphis, closer to her family for the first time in years and in the same small office as Grayson Roberts, she starts to question her job, her lack of home, and even her memories of her rocky past with the church.

Gray is intrigued by Adrian from the moment he sees her, and he's determined to get to the bottom of why this girl, who loves old movies and hums when she works, won't go to church with him. As they grow closer, he wants more too, but how can he convince her to stay in Memphis when she doesn't believe in home—or God? Can he use his own broken past to break through hers?

Get your copy here:

https://scrivenings.link/noplacelikehome

***Candy Cane Wishes and Saltwater Dreams***

*A collection of Christmas beach romances*

*by five multi-published authors.*

***Mistletoe Make-believe* by Amy Anguish** – Charlie Hill's family thinks his daughter Hailey needs a mom–to the point they won't get off his back until he finds her one. Desperate to be free from their nagging, he asks a stranger to pretend she's his girlfriend during the holidays. When romance author Samantha Arwine takes a working vacation to St. Simon's Island over Christmas, she never dreamed she'd be involved in a real-life romance. Are the sparks between her and Charlie real? Or is her imagination over-acting … again?

***A Hatteras Surprise* by Hope Toler Dougherty** –Ginny Stowe spent years tending a childhood hurt that dictated her college study and work. Can time with an island visitor with ties to her past heal lingering wounds and lead her toward a happy Christmas … and more? Ben Daniels intends to hire a new branch manager for a Hatteras Island bank, then hurry back to his promotion and Christmas in Charlotte. Spending time with a beautiful local, however, might force him to adjust his sails.

***A Pennie for Your Thoughts* by Linda Fulkerson** –When the Lakeshore Homeowner's Association threatens to condemn the cabin Pennie Vaughn inherited from her foster mother, her only hope of funding the needed repairs lies in winning a travel blog contest. Trouble is, Pennie never goes anywhere. Should she use the all-expenses paid Hawaiian vacation offered to her by her ex-fiancé? The trip that would have been their honeymoon?

***Mr. Sandman* by Regina Rudd Merrick** – Events manager Taylor Fordham's happily-ever-after was snatched from her, and she's saying no to romance and Christmas. When she meets two new friends—the cute new chef at Pilot Oaks and a contributor on a sci-fi fan fiction website who enjoys debate—her resolve begins to waver. Just when she thinks she can loosen her grip on thoughts of love, a crisis pulls her back. There's no way she's going to risk her heart again.

***Coastal Christmas* by Shannon Taylor Vannatter** – Lark Pendleton is banking on a high-society wedding to make her grandparent's inn at Surfside Beach, Texas the venue to attract buyers. Tasked with sprucing up the inn, she hires Jace Wilder, whose heart she once broke. When the bride and groom turn out to be Lark's high school nemesis and ex-boyfriend, she and Jace embark on a pretend romance to save the wedding. But when real feelings emerge, can they overcome past hurts?

Get your copy here:

***Saving Grace***

Michelle Wilson's one goal in life was to become a top journalist at the local paper back in her hometown of Cedar Springs, AR. But on the way to bringing that dream to reality, a life-changing wreck interrupts Michelle's plans and adds an orphaned baby into the mix. Now, she has tough decisions ahead—did God put her in that accident to save baby Grace? And if so, why is it so hard to convince everyone else she should be the baby's new mommy?

Greg Marshall has been Michelle's best friend his whole life. He's thrilled she's moving back home, but not so sure about her sudden desire to be a single mom. His feelings for her have grown through the years, but she's never seemed to notice. Can he help Michelle with the adoption and grow their relationship at the same time?

Get your copy here:

**Faith and Hope**

Hope needs more hope. Faith needs more faith. They both need a whole lot of love.

Two sisters. One summer. Multiple problems.

Younger sister Hope has lost her job, her car, and her boyfriend all in one day. Her well-laid plans for life have gone sideways, as has her hope in God.

Older sister Faith is finally getting her dream-come-true after years of struggles and prayers. But when her mom talks her into letting Hope move in for the summer, will the stress turn her dream into a nightmare? Is her faith in God strong enough to handle everything?

For two sisters who haven't gotten along in years, this summer together could be a disaster, or it could lead them to a closer relationship with each other and God. Can they overcome all life is throwing at them? Or is this going to destroy their relationship for good?

Get your copy here:

https://scrivenings.link/faithandhope

**An Unexpected Legacy**

When Chad Manning introduces himself to Jessica Garcia at her
favorite smoothie shop, it's like he stepped out of one of her romance
novels. But as she tentatively walks into a relationship with this man
of her dreams, secrets from their past threaten to shatter their
already fragile bond. Chad and Jessica must struggle to figure out if
their relationship has a chance or if there is nothing between them
but a love of smoothies.

Get your copy here:

https://scrivenings.link/anunexpectedlegacy

# MORE CONTEMPORARY ROMANCE
# FROM SCRIVENINGS PRESS

**Love in the Squared Circle**

**by Heather Greer**

Trinity Knight is not a fan of professional wrestling. But with her husband gone, it falls to her to give their son the father-son trip they daydreamed about when he was alive. After Trinity causes them to miss a meet and greet with Jay's favorite wrestler, a random act of kindness saves the trip and starts Trinity on an unexpected path.

Universal Wrestling Organization Champion Blane Sterling hears whiny children at photo ops all the time. However, overhearing a young boy comfort his mother piques his interest. Touched by their story, Blane works with the UWO Public Relations team to give Jay the experience of a lifetime.

As they learn each other's stories, Trinity and Blane are drawn to each other. But they don't just come from different states. They live in different worlds. Trinity might learn to fit into his life, but can those in her world look beyond Blane's profession to see his heart? Or will a lack of acceptance cause Trinity and Blane to lose their shot at love?

*Hope Takes the Reins*

**by Jenny Carlisle**

O.D. Billings has lived in the shadow of his brothers all his life. Even his name brings him down, so he has used only initials for years. Now, his older brother has returned home from the army, rejecting the role his family expects him to assume in their pickup truck dealership, and the younger brother is intent on risking his life on the back of a bucking bull. O.D.'s fans at the rodeo love his confident swagger during tie-down roping competitions, but every trail he heads down on his own seems to wind up going nowhere.

Hope Caldwell's world is still reeling after her mom's recent death from cancer. She thrives on keeping the family's rodeo business going. Getting back to normal seems impossible when she overhears her uncle's plans to sell out. How can she continue without the only way of life she has known for all of her nineteen years? Can she rely on the help of a big-talking cowboy? Or does he have too many problems of his own?

*Stay up-to-date on your favorite books and authors with our free e-newsletters.*

ScriveningsPress.com

Benjamin Smith can't quite figure out how he ended up a groomsman in two different weddings over the summer. But with his sister and a cousin both getting married, he's spending a lot of time at Happily Ever After events. Falling for a blonde who has no dreams of settling down wasn't in his five-year plan, yet the more he sees Skye, the more he wants to figure her out. But can she ever see him as anything more than a boring attorney and her complete opposite?

www.ingramcontent.com/pod-product-compliance
Lightning Source LLC
Chambersburg PA
CBHW070634100726
47907CB00007B/1981